DOCTOR WHO

The King's Dragon

The DOCTOR WHO series from BBC Books

Apollo 23 *by Justin Richards*

Night of the Humans *by David Llewellyn*

The Forgotten Army *by Brian Minchin*

Nuclear Time *by Oli Smith*

The King's Dragon *by Una McCormack*

The Glamour Chase *by Gary Russell*

DOCTOR WHO

The King's Dragon

UNA McCORMACK

BOOKS

1 3 5 7 9 10 8 6 4 2

Published in 2010 by BBC Books, an imprint of Ebury Publishing.
A Random House Group Company

Doctor Who is a BBC Wales production for BBC One.
Executive producers: Steven Moffat, Piers Wenger and Beth Willis

The Random House Group Limited Reg. No. 954009

Addresses for companies within the Random House Group can be found at
www.randomhouse.co.uk

A CIP catalogue record for this book is available from the British Library.

ISBN 978 1 846 07990 0

Mixed Sources
Product group from well-managed
forests and other controlled sources
www.fsc.org Cert no. TT-COC-2139
© 1996 Forest Stewardship Council

The Random House Group Limited supports the Forest Stewardship
Council (FSC), the leading international forest certification organisation.
All our titles that are printed on Greenpeace approved FSC certified
paper carry the FSC logo. Our paper procurement policy can be found
at www.rbooks.co.uk/environment

Commissioning editor: Albert DePetrillo
Series consultant: Justin Richards
Project editor: Steve Tribe
Cover design: Lee Binding © Woodlands Books Ltd, 2010
Production: Rebecca Jones

Printed and bound in Great Britain by Clays Ltd, St Ives PLC

For Matthew,
of course

'Woe for that man
who in harm and hatred hales his soul
to fiery embraces; nor favor nor change
awaits he ever.'
From *Beowulf* translated by Francis B. Gummere

They came only at night. They crept around the dark places, the hidden places, the poor and lonely places.

It was said in the city that you could tell when they approached. First your skin began to prickle and then a sickening cold fear lodged itself in your belly which rose and rose, up and up – until you could not speak and you could not breathe, and the lamp that you were carrying couldn't bear it any longer and went out – *phoomph!* And then the shadows grew thick and dark, and you could no longer see round the bend in the alley or the curve in the road. You could not see the peril that was lurking ahead, but it was there. And it lingered.

That's what was said. But when you asked the tale-bearer if he or she had seen these things themselves, 'Not I!' was the answer. But a cousin, or a cousin's friend, had heard the tale from someone else: 'A reputable source, mind you! My cousin is not one for telling tales!' And you would shake your head politely and reply, 'No, no! Of course!' But privately you would dismiss the story (again) and return to your business. For business was booming these days in Geath. All was well now that the city had its new young king.

Still, you might think, as you locked the doors, front and back, and you sealed up the windows, it was strange how empty the streets became after dusk. It was strange, too, how we all bolted our doors and our windows these days.

And each night, someone scurrying down a narrow alley or across a deserted plaza, on some business that sadly could not wait till the morning, would fancy that they could see shadows moving ahead, moving without any wind behind them, this summer being a hot one.

And some people – the most fanciful, surely, and the least trustworthy – would add a little colour to their tale. (For the best of us cannot resist a little colour.) There was a strange noise, they said, like the growl of a wild beast – and some would swear that on the wall of the passage curving ahead, they had seen the long shadow of a hand, or a claw, stretching out.

And the funny thing was, they would say, that this hand had too many fingers…

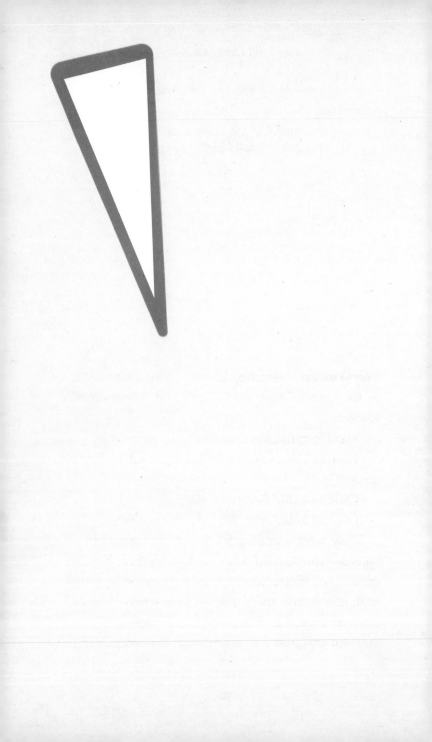

Chapter
1

'I don't know why I assumed an alien planet would be in the future,' Amy said, 'but I did. Flying cars. Rockets.'

'Food in pills,' Rory said.

'Food in pills, yes. But it's not like that at all. It's more…'

'Olde worlde?' Rory offered.

'Olde worlde,' Amy agreed. 'But not retro.'

They were standing by the side of the road – an olde-worlde road, without flagstones and with mud. A few metres ahead of them, the Doctor stood with one thumb stuck out, his face screwed up in concentration. He was staring at a horse and cart that, for the past five minutes, had been making steady progress down the track towards them. The driver's attention, however, was focused no further forwards than the ears of his horse.

'If I'm being honest,' Rory said, 'I didn't expect horses. Is there any particular reason to expect horses? On an alien planet, I mean? Or have I missed something?'

Amy gave it a couple of moments' thought. 'I don't think you've missed anything.'

The front of the cart was now almost level with the Doctor. He stuck his thumb out further; the universe's most intense hitchhiker. Slowly, ever so slowly, the cart rolled past. The golden bells on the harness jingled merrily.

Amy gave the driver a cheerful salute as he went on his way. 'Why, Doctor!' she cried. 'Is there *anything* you can't do?'

For the merest fraction of a second, the Doctor remained stretched out in his hitchhiking pose. He looked like a slightly forlorn scarecrow, or a particularly scruffy stork.

Abruptly, he turned on his heel and rejoined his friends. His trousers and shirt were splattered in mud. Brightly, he said, 'Beautiful day! Let's walk!'

The day was very hot for walking so they set a gentle pace. The afternoon ambled amiably towards evening and the sun slipped away, although it did not take the heat with it. As the travellers neared the top of the next hill, a yellow moon put in an appearance.

'Are we there yet?' Amy called forward.

The Doctor, two steps ahead as ever, said, 'Not long now.'

'I hope this place is something special, Doctor,' Amy said. She glanced at Rory, trudging behind her, his expression murderous. 'For your sake.'

'Top of the hill! Then you'll see why I've brought you here.' The Doctor – all frantic energy and hectic delight – reached the top of the hill and balanced precariously on a gravelly escarpment, throwing his arms out like a showman.

'The city of Geath!' he cried. 'Revered throughout the universe for the beauty of its buildings, the wisdom of its people, the excellence of its sauces – and, most of all, for the unlikely fact that, for twelve and a half thousand years, it has been at peace with its neighbouring cities. Its name is a byword for hospitality, craftsmanship and civilised conversation. Forget rockets and flying cars and food in pills – Geath is something truly remarkable. A bunch of people who not only don't see the point of getting into fights with each other, but have managed not to get into fights for about as a long as it took your species to get all the way from hitting each other on the head with clubs to nuclear bombs... Have I mentioned how good their sauces are?' He kissed the tips of his fingers. 'Nothing on your world comes close.'

Rory, struggling to keep his foothold on the stony slope, said, 'My nan makes good gravy.'

Amy's eyes went hazy with happy memory. 'Oh yes...'

'If you can bring yourselves back for a moment to the *alien planet* you're standing on,' the Doctor said, 'and if you ever make it to the top of this hill, I promise you will see a sight capable of putting thought even of Sunday lunch out of your head.'

He reached out a hand, Amy took it, and reached back to Rory in turn. Together they took the last step up. The clouds in the sky parted and the light from the setting sun made the valley below them glow.

Amy gasped.

Rory said, 'Wow.'

The Doctor smiled. 'Exactly.'

In the valley below, a long river wound lazily in a great curve and, in this bend, lay the city of Geath. It dazzled. Amy blinked, to little effect, and was obliged to shield her eyes with her hand to be able to make out the shape of the city.

It spread up from the river onto hills that lay to the north in a grand display. It was as if the people of the city had no fear of showing their beautiful home to the wider world. In fact, they wanted everyone to see. And why not? It glowed in the sunset; the late light caught upon the red tiles of the roofs, the yellow buildings, the gold…

As Amy looked more closely, she was able to pick out detail. The city was laid out in circles: concentric avenues running in rings that drew her eye to a central plaza. There, in the heart of the city, stood a huge round building with a great domed roof.

The dome was golden. Amy reached out her hand as if to touch it. It was a marvel, smooth and round and precious, like the egg of a magical creature. Amy wanted to run her hand across its surface and feel the sun-tinged metal in her hand.

'Like it?' said the Doctor.

'It's the most beautiful thing I've ever seen,' Amy replied.

Rory, in a quiet awed voice, said, 'What *is* that place?'

'The council chamber,' the Doctor said. 'The heart of Geath, where its citizens meet to debate, discuss, deliberate – and eat.' He checked his watch, tapped its face, then checked it again. 'We should get a move on.'

Rory was already halfway down the hill. Amy half-ran and half-slid after him, eager for a proper look at the astonishing golden hall. Could it be as glorious up close? Could anything? Turning to look back, she saw the Doctor standing still on the hilltop, hands stuck in his pockets. Behind him, it was starting to get dark.

'Come on!' she called.

The Doctor nodded, as if coming to a decision, and followed her and Rory down the hill. They still had some way to go.

As she walked, it occurred to Amy that the driver of that cart had not shown much of the reputed hospitality. But it was hardly worth mentioning. No doubt they looked like a fairly odd bunch of hitchhikers. She couldn't really blame him for passing them by.

The track down the hill and their new enthusiasm soon brought them to the broad paved road that led into Geath. They crossed the river by means of a great stone bridge. It was obviously ancient, but immaculately constructed; the massive blocks smooth and interlocking. The sun set, but the evening remained hot, making the promise of the grand hall and a friendly welcome even more appealing. It was very quiet. Nobody passed them, walking or riding, in either direction.

Ten more minutes brought the travellers to an arched gate in the city walls. The walls were very high and the gate very locked. Behind them, everything was quiet. A single torch glowed dimly and they huddled under it.

'Have we got here after closing time?' Amy asked.

'Closing time? In Geath? No such thing.'

'A locked gate isn't very hospitable,' Rory said.

'No.' The Doctor looked thoughtfully at it. 'Odd, isn't it?'

'Maybe if we let them know we're here they'll be all smiles,' Amy said.

She reached for the hammer on the door. It was a fascinating design: it looked like a dragon, clambering up the gate, its head turned sideways so that a single ruby red eye could keep watch on the road leading up to the city. The dragon's long gold tail curled down to form the door-knocker. Amy picked up the tail – then dropped it, quickly.

'Doctor, it's warm!'

The Doctor unfurled a long finger and, tentatively, brushed the tip along the dragon's tail. 'So it is.'

Amy reached to take hold of it again but the Doctor was there first. She tutted in annoyance. Why couldn't she be the one to experiment for once? Out came the sonic screwdriver. Hadn't she seen it first? Amy watched unhappily as the Doctor ran his thumb down the scales on the dragon, almost caressing them.

'Definitely odd,' he said. Then he picked up the long tail and banged it hard against the gate.

There was a pause, a thump, and then somebody cursed inventively. The spy-hole in the gate opened.

The Doctor stuck his face up close and grinned through. 'Hello! How are you? Can we come in?'

'Who's there? What do you want?'

The Doctor fumbled in his pocket and pulled out his psychic paper. He held it up closer to the hole in the gate.

The keeper muttered a reply.

'Sorry,' the Doctor said. 'Having a bit of trouble hearing you! Big wooden gate in the way!'

'I said I can't read!'

'Ah.' The Doctor stared down at the paper. 'Of course. Oral culture. That's a design flaw, isn't it?'

There was another series of thumps from behind the gate, which then opened a crack.

'But the wife can,' said the gatekeeper. 'So you'd better come in.' He peered behind the Doctor and shook his head at Amy and Rory. 'Not them. Only you.'

The Doctor went through the gate, unapologetically looking back over his shoulder at his friends.

They stood there for almost two whole minutes before Amy muttered, 'Bored now!' She waved at

Rory. 'Come on, then. Leg up.'

'What?'

'If they won't let me in through the gate, I'm going over the wall.'

'Amy, can't you wait for once?'

'Not a chance!'

'But what if they don't let the Doctor through? Then you'll be stuck in there—'

Patiently, Amy explained. 'No – I'll be on the inside and can come and open the gate once the keeper has gone back into his house. Hands, please.'

About three and a half seconds later, Rory was crouching with his hands clasped together in front of him. Amy was standing on them and scrabbling up the wall.

'Sometimes,' Rory said to Amy's left shin, 'I feel like I've spent my entire life doing things like this. And then I start to worry that I'm going to spend the rest of my life doing things like this... Amy! That's my face you're standing on!'

'Nothing vital, then.'

'Thanks a lot!' He pushed her up, she pushed too – and then she was sitting on top of the wall. A sudden thought struck him. 'Amy – what do we do if the Doctor *does* persuade them to open the gate?'

'What?'

'There'll only be one of us. One of me! Here! By myself!'

Amy grinned down at him. 'You'll think of something. You usually do.' Then she swung over the wall and was gone.

Inevitably, the gate opened a split-second later. The Doctor breezed out with the gatekeeper scurrying behind him.

'No need to apologise! Easy mistake to make!' the Doctor said cheerily. Then he saw Rory, standing by himself, and frowned.

The gatekeeper tapped the Doctor's arm. 'Excuse me for asking, but I thought you said two companions?'

'So I did,' the Doctor replied.

'She... got tired and went home,' Rory offered.

The Doctor rolled his eyes. 'You mentioned a carriage?' he said to the gatekeeper, as Rory came sheepishly through the gate.

'On its way,' the gatekeeper said. 'Don't want you wandering around the city at night, do we?'

'Don't we?' said the Doctor.

'Well, dark night, empty streets, you never know who's hanging around.'

The Doctor scratched his nose. 'Don't you?'

'Still, better than it used to be. Time was anyone could walk into Geath, any time, day or night! Can you believe it?'

He swung the gate closed. It gave a loud thump, as the Doctor said, softly, 'Why is that a bad thing?'

Amy slipped round to the back of the gatehouse. She could hear the Doctor speaking – quickly, so that the gatekeeper (and, presumably, his wife) didn't get much of a chance – but she couldn't make out any words. Never mind. As long as the Doctor was talking, he'd be keeping them busy and away from her. She inched around the side of the house, coming to a halt near a window. Slowly, she leaned forwards to peer inside.

The room was crammed full of gold. The candlesticks were made of gold. The poker and fire-irons were made of gold. The door handle – yes, that looked a lot like gold. There was gold stitching on the curtains and on the cloth that covered the small table below the window upon which cutlery (gold) and plate (gold) were laid out. All of it gleamed in the candlelight. Two comfortable chairs stood facing each other companionably. Gold cushions rested plumply upon them. It was a tiny, very cosy treasure vault.

'What,' Amy muttered to the absent gatekeeper, 'is your scam, exactly?'

She tried the window. It opened. Carefully, still listening out for the conversation going on round the front of the building, Amy leaned inside, exactly far enough to be able to touch one of the spoons on the table. It too was warm. More than that, it was…

Wriggling.

'Whoa!' Amy jerked back her hand. 'Now that is the most freakish thing in a whole world of freakishness!'

She was about to test it again, but the conversation at the front of the house was finishing. Quickly, she pulled the window down again and slipped back into the shadow of the wall.

The gate was open. Rory slunk in, tail between his legs.

'Poor Rory,' Amy whispered to him. 'I'm guessing you didn't think of something.'

She edged round to the road, keeping to the shadows. The Doctor was gabbling away, at the gatekeeper and his wife. Then a carriage pulled up. A golden carriage.

'How lucky you are,' gushed the gatekeeper's wife, as Rory and the Doctor clambered into their carriage. 'You're going to meet the King! The King!'

'King?' Rory whispered to the Doctor, as they took their seats. 'I thought this was a republic or something.'

'It is. It *was*.' The Doctor leaned over to open the door on the other side of the carriage. Amy hopped in. 'Hurry up!' said the Doctor. 'We're going to meet the King!'

'King?' Amy nodded back towards the gatehouse. 'You should see how the other half lives.'

The carriage clattered along. The Doctor frowned out of the window, beyond which the city of Geath gleamed silently. Rory and Amy waited patiently.

Eventually, the Doctor held up some fingers. 'There are three things wrong here. Firstly, as Rory pointed out, the people of Geath don't have a king. They have a council. They have elections. They have made an *art form* out of elections. That's the first thing wrong.'

One of the Doctor's fingers went down. He stopped talking and resumed frowning. Amy and Rory exchanged a look.

The carriage continued through the deserted city. They went down long curved avenues, through little plazas with statues and fountains at the centre, caught glimpses of covered steps leading up the hill and alleyways leading down to the river – but they saw nobody. The carriage rattled into a plaza bigger than any they had passed through yet and far more elaborately gilded. The torchlight glittered on the thick metal that coated the fronts of the buildings. A deep-noted bell gonged; once, twice.

Amy jumped. 'This place is giving me the creeps.'

Crossing the plaza, the carriage came to a halt. The travellers climbed out and found themselves in front of a huge round building. This had to be the hall they had seen from the hilltop, Amy thought; the one with the magical dome. That was too high for her to see it clearly; looking up she saw instead a haze of soft light rising above the hall. The walls of the building were enamelled; the decoration more intricate than anything she had seen so far, with swirling spiral patterns that bewildered her eye when she looked for more than a few seconds. Two men stood on guard in front of the hall's big arched doors. There was nobody else in sight. Silence enveloped the city, a watchful, anxious silence. The night heat was cloying. Amy looked at the golden hall and gave a shudder of trepidation.

'The second thing that's wrong,' the Doctor said, 'is that the streets are empty. Geathians live their lives out in the streets and the plazas. Daytime: they sit outside and work and talk. Night-time: they sit outside and eat and talk. So where is everyone? Why are they hiding away and locking their doors?' He put one more finger down.

The two guards came towards them, bowed low, and gestured at them to come inside. They walked into a wide white corridor with an arched roof; there were alcoves at intervals along each wall, and in each of these some golden artefact was on display: vases, statues, figures clasping gilded lamps. The further in they went, the more lavish these objects became, as if they were drawing nearer and nearer to the source of it all.

'The *third* thing that's wrong,' said the Doctor, 'and, speaking for myself, I think this probably comes under the heading "most wrong" – is that gold doesn't occur naturally on this world. Not an ingot, not a leaf, not a flake. There shouldn't be any gold.' He glanced back down the corridor. 'But there is. There's *quite a lot* of gold.'

They came to a pair of double doors. One of the guards pushed these open, and the companions walked through into a huge chamber, full of light and music and people. The Doctor still had one finger raised. It stayed raised and, as Amy watched, those closest to them began to notice. They fell silent; they nudged the next group along, who looked round and, seeing the Doctor, also fell silent. The clamour of conversation lessened steadily and the music faltered. Soon the hall was in complete silence and everybody in it was looking their way.

The Doctor waggled his finger in greeting. 'Hello! I'm the Doctor. No, don't get up.'

Chapter

2

A chamber full of courtiers glared at them. The Doctor beamed back, his smile like a ray of pure white light through the hostile, shimmering room. Hundreds of people were gathered there, glorious in their finery, as if the jewel-drenched and fantastic figures of a mosaic had stepped down and taken shape in the real world.

Amy looked around in amazement. If the gatehouse had been stuffed with gold, this place was smothered in it.

'Blimey,' Rory whispered. 'Bling Central.'

Suddenly, as if someone had breathed life into them, or turned their key, the courtiers began to move apart, as methodically as dancers, half of them shifting to one side of the great round chamber, half to the other. As they moved, the heart of the hall was slowly revealed: the source of the glamour, the place from which it all sprang.

Raised up on a dais, apart from the rest of the gathering, a young man sat on a golden throne. He was tall and strong and handsome, and he wore a narrow circlet of gold around his head. Standing at his right shoulder, tactfully behind him, was another man. He was only slightly older, although his dark clothes were very severe, and he looked almost nondescript compared to everyone else in the hall. The only decoration he wore was on his left hand, which was covered in fabulous rings. These two men, however, were not quite the star attraction. Curled up in front of the throne, one red eye fixed upon the entrance of the chamber and thus upon the travellers, was a huge, sinuous, golden dragon.

'So... which one's the King?' whispered Amy.

Rory turned his laugh into a cough. The Doctor raised a remonstrative eyebrow.

The silence stretched on, charged and distinctly unwelcoming. Then the older of the two men leaned forwards and whispered something in the King's ear. The young man burst out laughing. So did the Doctor. Within seconds the whole room was in uproar, from the gaudiest toady to the lowliest hanger-on.

The King clapped his hands together. The room fell instantly silent. He rose up from his throne, taller than everyone around him, stronger, confident of his beauty and his power. He was like a lazy, well-fed lion, muscular and commanding.

'Nice,' Amy said, appreciatively.

The King smiled down at the new arrivals. 'To our friends and neighbours,' he said, 'I, Beol, King of Geath, offer a most hearty welcome. Come, my friends! Come and join me! Come and speak with me!'

'Hooray!' cried the Doctor. 'All friends! Marvellous! Amy, let's go and pay our respects to our host. Rory,' he put his hand against Rory's shoulder and gave him a gentle shove, 'mingle.' His voice dropped. 'And *listen*. Both of you.'

'Neighbours, Doctor?' Amy muttered, as they made their way through the curious whispering crowd.

'Oh, the psychic paper, you know,' he said offhandedly. Reaching the foot of the dais, he swept out an outrageous bow. 'Friend! Lord! King of Geath! *Love* what you've done with the place – and *what*,' he spun round to look at the dragon, 'do we have here?'

The man behind the throne jumped forwards. 'Don't touch it!'

The Doctor's long hands, bare millimetres away from a great golden haunch of dragon, swung up again, palms out. 'All right, won't touch. Hey, nice rings! Who are you?'

'He's my Teller,' Beol said. He seemed to be entertained by the scene unfolding in front of him.

'Teller, Doctor?' Amy murmured.

'Oh, you know,' the Doctor said. 'Oral cultures – always someone whose job it is to do the memorising and the storytelling. Not to mention the spin-doctoring.'

'So nothing to do with counting the cash?'

'Not usually. But then there's a lot of "not usually" going on around here. A whole heap. A hoard. This is Amy, by the way,' he said to Beol. 'Amy, say hello to the King.'

Amy lifted her hand to hip-height and gave a little wave. 'Um… hello.'

Beol, in return, delivered up a heart-stopping smile.

'Wow,' Amy said. 'And we get Prince Charles.'

'That's aristocracies for you,' said the Doctor. 'You never know what's going to come out. Bit like a tombola. Where did you say you'd found this dragon?'

'We didn't,' said the Teller. 'Where did you say you'd come from?'

'Dant, wasn't it?' said the King. Something was definitely amusing him.

The Doctor produced another ludicrous bow. 'From the people of Dant, greetings and all the best and, um, cheers. So – the dragon? Can't be many of these lying around. Where did you dig this one up?'

Beol turned to his Teller and gave him an odd smile. 'Why don't you tell them?'

There seemed to be some private joke going on between them, although the Teller wasn't laughing. He looked put out.

'Be seated, my friends,' Beol said to the Doctor and Amy. 'He tells this tale so very well.'

He clapped his hands again. Servants carried up two ornate chairs onto the dais. Beol gestured to them to sit down.

'Last question for the moment, Doctor,' Amy said, as they took their seats. 'Dant?'

'Don't know… Hang on, yes I do, next city along. Up the river and left a bit.'

'And that's where we're from?'

'Apparently.' He gave her his lopsided grin. 'Citizens of Dant, though! Well done us!'

'I know!'

'Noticed anything yet?'

'Yes. That dragon. Is it me, or is it, sort of, oozing? Or something?'

The Doctor's smile switched off. 'It's not you.'

Rory drifted obediently through the room and listened to the conversation. He soon realised that everyone was talking about the same thing. Beol. Who had seen Beol, who had spoken to Beol, what Beol said, how he said it, and what he was wearing at the time. Not all of what Rory heard had the ring of truth and, in fact, the further away he got from the centre of the hall, the more fanciful the stories became and the more they carried with them the distinct whiff of desperation. 'Help,' Rory muttered. 'I'm a prisoner in *Heat* magazine.' He inched his way to the edge of the crowd and looked for a quiet spot where he could observe people in peace.

A covered arcade ran around the perimeter of the room, providing a haven for those who found the bustle close to the dais too much. Chairs and tables had been placed between its columns. These were mostly deserted, apart from one, at which an old woman sat, alone. Her chin was propped up on her hands and she stared out across the hall with a bored expression. Seeing that Rory was looking at her, she gestured to him to join her. When he got close, she rose up from her seat and, with some ceremony, pulled out a chair for him.

'Hello,' Rory said, as he sat down. 'I'm Rory.'

Why did it sound better when the Doctor said it?

The old woman gave a brisk nod of the head. 'And I'm Hilthe. Welcome to Geath.'

'Thank you.'

'I haven't seen you here before,' she said.

'I haven't been here before. First time in Geath.'

'Yes? Then tell me, Rory, what do you think of my city?'

Rory gazed out across the chamber at the glamorous gathering and then up at the shimmering light-filled dome. He could not see Beol, or the dragon, but he knew they were there, and he could easily picture how magnificent they both looked. 'I think it's amazing.'

Hilthe reached for a bottle and another glass. 'I think it's tasteless.'

The glass chinked against the bottle. Rory blinked. Suddenly everything around him seemed garish and flashy. The gold was a slick coating over the hall's true beauties. When Rory peered past it, he was able to see how the hall had once appeared. Pale stone and subtle frescoes; measured and delicate. 'That's the trouble with bling.'

'Bling?'

Rory gestured around them. 'All this stuff. Showy. You know.'

'*Bling*.' Hilthe rolled the word around, trying

it out. 'I like that. I'll remember it.' She pushed a glass towards him. 'Drink up. It makes the evening pass more quickly.'

From the centre of the hall, applause broke out. It rippled outwards, until soon the people standing at the edge near their table were clapping and pressing forwards. Hilthe sighed. 'Here comes our bedtime story. Same story, every night. And every night, they hang on the Teller's every word. They've all gone quite mad.' Her voice took on a note of cheerful desperation. 'Or I'm getting old. Or both.'

'The same story? What's it about?'

'How brave Beol won the dragon and brought it to Geath.' She spoke violently, almost viciously. That was when Rory noticed she wasn't wearing any gold. 'What else could we possibly want to hear about?'

Rory got up from his seat to look over the crowd, trying to see what was happening in the centre of the hall. The older man, the one who had been standing behind the King – the Teller, presumably – walked to the front of the dais. He made a brief show of reluctance but the crowd cheered him on. From deep within the hall, a chant arose, taken up by everyone until it boomed around the dome. It was the King's name: *Beol! Beol! Beol!*

'See what I mean?' Hilthe said. 'They've all

gone mad.'

The man lifted up his left hand. The rings on it glittered sharply in the lamplight. The crowd fell silent. 'So,' he said, and then paused for effect.

Hilthe groaned and reached for her bottle. 'Here we go again…'

The Tale of the King and the Dragon

'Hear now,' said the Teller, 'great men and women gathered here in the heart-hall of Geath, how *Beol*—'

Hearing the name, the crowd said, 'Ah!'

'How Beol, of all men bravest and boldest, haled to this high hall a gift of great worth—' The Teller flung out his arm.

'Ooh!' said the crowd.

' — hear now how Sheal was shorn of the golden worm—'

'Is he alliterating?' whispered Amy to the Doctor.

'It's the form. It's how it's done. Shush! Want to listen.'

Amy settled back in her chair and got comfortable. The hall was very full and very warm. The light from the lamps and the torches filled the place with a soft gold haze that imbued it with a dreamy feeling. Amy closed her eyes.

When you listened carefully, she thought, the

Teller's voice had a lot going for it. He used it like a musical instrument – one moment dropping down to a whisper that made Amy lean in to catch his words, the next moment bellowing out a war cry and making her jump back. There was something else too – his voice conjured up vivid images in her mind. She could picture in detail everything he described – not like television, little images flickering away in the corner of the room – this was more immediate, more immersive, like a lucid dream. It swept you up and carried you along. Amy followed the Teller as he led her through Beol's deeds: she gasped at the King's audacity, tricking his way into the city of Sheal; she laughed herself nearly into hiccups to hear the way he made such fools out of the townsfolk; she chewed her nails at the suspense of him creeping through the city; and she thrilled at the knockdown fight with the guards. And then he laid hands upon the dragon...

Amy opened her eyes. There it was, lying at the heart of the city, the red slit of its eye watching, its mouth curved in a hungry smile. The Teller's tale went on without her. Amy leaned forwards in her chair, mesmerised by the hugeness of the dragon and the beauty of it. She marvelled at the craft that must have gone into each scale upon its back, the long flat ears, the elegant snout, the humming...

Humming? Amy shook her head. Yes, she could hear humming: a faint and distant chord that was pitched perfectly with the Teller's rich tones. Was it the musicians, accompanying him? Amy listened more closely. No, it was too precise for that. This sound was mechanical… Amy strained to listen. And then she heard something else – behind the Teller's voice, behind the dragon's music. A whisper in her mind, inchoate and almost suppressed, but she could just make out the sense of it. The whisper said: *Will it come back tonight? Will the monster come back tonight?*

Monster? Fear clawed at Amy and she began to tremble. She looked round the room, but she could only see strangers, alien strangers on an alien world. She was quite alone.

Suddenly, the Teller's voice swooped up in anger. Amy jumped. He was describing the pursuit of Beol made by the people of Sheal in their anger at the theft of the dragon. They chased him like a vagabond up hill and down dale, set their dogs after him ('Boo!' hissed the crowd), but at last he came to Geath, and he brought the dragon with him. But Sheal was angry. The crowd shivered in fear at this threat – but then the Teller soothed them, reminded them how Beol had won once and would win again. Beol was their King, he said. Beol would protect them.

'Amy. Amy.' Someone spoke softly in her ear, breaking the spell. It was the Doctor. 'What is it? Can you hear something?'

The tale ended. The crowd broke into rapturous applause. *Beol!* they cried. *Beol! Beol!* The name dispelled all fear. Amy shook her head. 'I heard nothing.' And what had she heard, really – a whisper, a hum, a story? She nodded at the Teller. 'He's good, isn't he?'

Hilthe sat up with sudden interest. 'Now this is new! Whenever he's told this story before, he's always said that Beol won the dragon from the people of Dant. But this time it's from the people of Sheal. I wonder what that could mean...' Hilthe glanced round the hall and shook her head. 'Not that it makes any difference to this lot. I doubt anyone else has even noticed. He could tell them they brought it back from the moon and they'd believe him.'

'Is any of the story true?' Rory asked.

'Some of it. They did ride into town with that dragon on a cart behind them. Quite an old cart – one of the wheels was about to fall off. From the way he tells it now you'd think it was a chariot, with half a hundred acrobats behind.'

'What happened next?'

'We assumed at first that they were showmen.

And then Beol challenged me to debate with him. Which I did and, after that, we did what we do best. We held an election. Which Beol won – and I lost.'

There was a whole world of disappointment compressed into those few words. 'I'm sorry,' Rory said gently.

Hilthe patted his hand. 'Thank you. Very kind of you. Once I would have said that such is the nature of things, that fortune's wheel can turn in an instant – but immediately the city began to change. Not only in appearance – although that is certainly startling enough – but in the way it talked. Beol stopped being Councillor and instead was called King. And then we began to hear that the people of Dant and Sheal and Jutt were jealous of us and our new wealth, and that we must be watchful, and trust Beol to protect us...'

On the dais, the Teller brought his story to a close. The crowd burst into rapturous applause. The King rose and bowed and left the hall, the Teller close behind.

Hilthe watched them go. 'And so Beol will protect us, the Teller says. Protect us from whom? We have never needed protecting in the past.'

Now that the King had gone, the courtiers left, flowing quickly past the table at which Hilthe and Rory sat. Beol's name was on everyone's lips; Beol's daring, Beol's courage. Hilthe sighed. 'It is very strange to watch people you have known and loved all the long years of your life change so swiftly into strangers. Perhaps I missed something? Perhaps they can see something that I cannot see?'

The room was almost empty. It felt tawdry and cold. Hilthe looked lost and sad. Rory pressed her hand. 'I don't think you missed anything. I think you're the only one seeing straight.'

A smile returned to the corners of the old woman's mouth and some sparkle to her eyes. 'Young man, I entirely agree with you!' As she got up to leave, Hilthe reached into her purse and brought out a small circular piece of tile. 'Thank you,' she said. 'If you don't mind listening to an old woman talk about the good old days – come and find me. I can talk about the good old days for ever.' She handed him the tile, bowed her head in farewell, and then ducked into the shadows of the arcade, leaving by another route to avoid the crowd.

A complex of rooms surrounded the council chamber, and the three travellers were assigned a suite a short walk away from the hall.

The Doctor checked the corridor outside, and then turned to his companions. 'Right. Pockets.' Amy and Rory stared at him blankly. 'I'll go first, shall I?' The Doctor removed his jacket. He brushed fruitlessly at some of the mud spatters, turned the jacket upside down and gave it a shake.

Gold poured onto the bed. Coins. Chains. A couple of forks. Another shake. Another fork. The Doctor picked it up and wondered at it. 'Forks… forks… what is it about forks all of a sudden?' He nodded at Rory. 'Your turn.'

Slowly, Rory emptied his pockets. Coins. More coins. A couple of rings. A few bracelets. 'Nice,' said the Doctor. 'Not really your style. Amy? What do you have for us?'

Amy stared at the treasure in disbelief. 'I don't know what you two have been up to, but I've not spent the whole evening pilfering!'

The Doctor shrugged. 'Check your pockets. You never know what might have fallen into them.'

'Nothing has "fallen into" my pockets!'

'Give it a go anyway.'

With much reluctance, Amy shoved her hand into a pocket – and pulled out a spoon. It was the one from the gatehouse. Amy stared down at it, warm in her hand. She had no recollection of picking it up. Under oath, she would have sworn she had only touched it.

'Try your other pocket.' The Doctor was watching her closely, his deep-set eyes dark and intense. Amy pulled out a necklace. She pooled

43

it into her palm. 'I don't even remember seeing this!'

'I'm sure you don't,' the Doctor replied. 'I don't remember much after the first fork and I was concentrating.' He took the necklace from her hand and added it to the pile. He hopped onto the bed and sat cross-legged, hunched over the loot, stirring it around with one finger. 'What about the rest?' he said. 'What are we not telling each other?'

'What do you mean?' said Rory.

'We were there for about two hours—'

'Really?' Amy was startled. She hadn't noticed the time pass.

'Mm. So think. What did you see? What did you hear?'

'There was a king and a dragon...' Amy said slowly. She laughed. 'You were there – you could hardly miss the pair of them!'

The Doctor took out his sonic screwdriver and switched it on, directing it at the gold. 'A king and a dragon. Anything else?'

'I got talking to an old woman...' Mid-sentence, Rory seemed to change his mind about what he was going to say. 'Doesn't matter, it wasn't that interesting.'

Under the sonic screwdriver's pale beam, the metal began to shift and change and liquefy. A haze gathered over it, like mist over the moon. 'The Teller told us how Beol won the dragon – hey, he was good, wasn't he?' Amy said, but as she spoke she remembered something else, something on the very edge of her memory, something that filled her with dread… She shook her head. No. That was rubbish. That was because the Teller was good at what he did. Like a scary movie. 'Oh, Doctor, you were sitting right next to me, you heard everything I did!'

'Yes. Yes, I did.' The Doctor switched off the sonic. The glow around the treasure disappeared. 'It's not gold, of course,' he said. 'There isn't any gold on Geath. I won't bore you with the full technical name because it would take the best part of two minutes to say it. Besides, it's more famous under its trade name. *Enamour.*'

The Doctor unfolded himself from his sitting position and picked up his jacket. He gave his jacket another shake which didn't result in any more treasure and didn't remove any more mud. 'And when I say "famous", what I mean is "infamous". Enamour is banned throughout all self-respecting galactic civilisations and in most of the disreputable ones too. It's advanced and highly dangerous technology, and what it's doing on a pre-industrial world like this I don't know.' He laid his jacket out carefully on the bed in front of him and stared down as if it was a particularly difficult puzzle. Then he shoved his arms into the sleeves and flung it back over the top of his head. Somehow, he ended up wearing it. 'But I want to take a closer look at that dragon. Find out where it came from.' He turned to his friends. 'Are you coming or are you staying?'

'Um...' said Rory. 'When you say "dangerous"...?'

'I mean dangerous – and not in a safe way. Are you coming?'

Amy laughed. 'What do you think?' She was first to the door – which meant she was first through it when the howling started in the corridor beyond.

Chapter
3

Outside, the corridor was dark, apart from a single lamp on the wall where the passage bent away towards the right. That was still burning, but as Amy watched, its flame withered and died. The howl grew louder. The low growl rose quickly in pitch until it was an eldritch shriek that made Amy's teeth tingle. Whatever was making all this racket was round the bend in the corridor.

Amy ran after it. As she swung round the corner, she saw the lamps gutter and die, one by one, plunging the way ahead into shadow. The screech stopped. Behind her, Rory shouted, 'Amy! Where are you? Wait!' But the lamps were going out more quickly, so she gathered pace and ran to catch up with the darkness. She heard the growl again, coming from ahead, rising up and drowning out Rory's voice.

Then the walls fell away from her. The howling stopped. 'Hello?' Amy called out, her voice echoing slightly. 'Who's there?' She peered ahead and, as her eyes adjusted, she saw that she was standing in a chamber about a quarter of the size of the council hall, as far as she could tell. A meeting place, perhaps, or a reception room. Nearby, a single lamp burned bravely. Through its slender light Amy glimpsed pale frescoes, ghostly figures dancing on the walls and, deep in the gloom, the glitter of gold, or Enamour, or whatever it was the Doctor called it. Beyond that, the room was completely dark, although, at the edge of her perception, she was sure something was moving, scratching, growling...

Amy took a deep breath. 'Right. Time for a closer look.' She lifted the lamp from its holding and, heart pounding, took a slow step forward. She held the light up and out in front of her, trying to get some real sense of what lay ahead. Two steps, three... and then the torch she was carrying began to flicker. 'Don't even think about it!' she told it.

But the lamp had its own plans – or, rather, something had plans for the lamp. Because it didn't simply go out – it was *pulled* out. To Amy's astonishment, the flame spun into a long thin golden thread, which was dragged across the room, where it was ravelled up and soon gone. 'Now that is just not fair!'

Deep in the darkness, whatever-it-was moved: two quick steps across the tiled floor. Amy jumped away, crashing to a halt when her back hit the wall of the chamber. The howl was low and rumbling and definitely a threat; a threat that was gaining ground, like an air-raid siren warning you of the approach of something terrible. It was a sound to keep you awake at night. More steps towards where Amy stood. Then she saw it, half-visible, barely a condensation of the darkness itself.

It was humanoid but elongated. Its limbs were thin and stretched, like the long black branches of a tree in winter, and they were growing longer. The creature's reach extended rapidly, spreading out from its side of the chamber towards Amy. She held her dead lamp up in front of her, a poor useless shield. To the shadow, she said, 'So there really is a monster. You'd think I'd know better by now. Hello, monster!'

Its jaws hinged open and it screamed back.

'Not much of a talker, eh? That's fine. I don't mind doing the talking.'

Its huge metalled arm stretched out towards her, scaled like the hide of a dragon. Amy held the lamp aloft. 'I come in peace!'

The creature unfurled its long fingers, too many fingers. Amy flinched back against the wall. 'Um... *help*?'

None came. But, as the first flood of emergency adrenalin subsided a little, Amy realised that lack of help might be less of a problem than she feared. The beast loomed darkly over her. Yes, it was big; yes, it was scary; yes, it was making enough of a noise that any second the dead were going to wake up and knock on the wall and complain about the racket and ask why a hard-working corpse couldn't get any sleep around here – but it wasn't actually coming any *closer*... If anything, it was keeping a slight distance; studying her, examining her...

Slowly, tentatively, Amy reached out to touch the creature in front of her. Her hand went right through it. The insubstantial giant shuddered, flickered half-in and half-out of sight, and then vanished.

All the lamps came back on, fiercely. Amy nearly dropped the one she was holding. Carefully, hands shaking, she put it back in its place on the wall, scolding it as she did so. 'Where were you when I needed you most?' With the lamp back in place, and breathing deeply to steady herself, she turned to take a look round. The room was empty, apart from the big stash of gold heaped up in the middle, gleaming prettily under the lamps.

Amy shook her head. 'Huh.' She went over to the gold. Cups and goblets; rings and brooches. Beautiful. She picked up one of the brooches. It had a lovely sheen about it, almost an aura, something that seemed separate from and yet at the same time intrinsic to the metal. She turned it over in her hands. It felt soft, like silk rippling between her fingers. And it was so very lovely... She was fixing the brooch to her jacket when Rory burst into the room.

'Amy!' He ran over to her. 'All you all right? What happened?'

Amy admired the brooch and then picked up a necklace from the top of the pile. 'Hmm?'

'What happened?'

She gave him a puzzled look. 'Nothing happened. The lights went out. I came in here and found some gold. Enamour. Whatever. Do you like my brooch?'

'What? Yes, it's very nice. Amy, what about the noise?'

'What noise?'

'You know!' Rory shrieked. 'That noise.'

'Oh, that.' Amy shrugged. 'I don't know. The wind, maybe. Trapped in the corridor. These old buildings, no proper insulation. Do you think this necklace is too much with the brooch?'

'The wind?' Rory was unconvinced. 'Do you think so?'

'Rory,' she said impatiently, 'if there was anything else, then I'd tell you, wouldn't I. OK?' She decided the necklace worked, put it on, and turned to go. Then she saw the Doctor.

He was standing by the door, leaning back against the wall, tapping the sonic screwdriver against his cheek. He was frowning. Tall and thin and alien, much scarier than any creeping shadow or sleeping dragon. Amy looked away, suddenly feeling 7 years old again and knowing that the stranger in the garden with the box of delights was disappointed in her. And then she felt cross with him, not only for leaving that 7-year-old behind after promising to be back, but because he didn't believe her now. She lifted her chin and looked him straight in the eye. 'There was nothing actually there,' she said firmly. 'It was all a trick of the light.'

The Doctor pushed himself up from the wall. 'All right,' he said pleasantly. He slipped the sonic screwdriver into his pocket. 'Well, as I was saying before we were so rudely interrupted, I'd like a closer look at that dragon.'

'Won't there be a guard on it?' Rory said. 'They're not going to let us wander in and take a poke at their precious dragon, are they?'

'When did that ever stop us?' Amy said, lightly. She walked past the Doctor and out of the chamber without meeting his eye again. 'Coming, boys?'

They came. The three of them crept back through the complex to the council chamber. Amy walked slightly behind and tried to clear her thoughts. 'No,' she said eventually, more to herself than anyone else, her fingers tangled in her new necklace. 'It was definitely a trick of the light. Too much imagination in the dark.'

'That's what you said before,' Rory replied.

'Because if the wind was howling around the corridors, it could have blown the lamps out, too, couldn't it? Couldn't it have been the wind?'

'Yes, the wind could have blown the lights out.'

So whatever she had seen – if in fact she had seen anything at all – it must have been her imagination. Yes, her imagination. This was what happened when you hung around with the Doctor. You started to believe there were monsters in every corridor, when it was only some wind rattling at the windows. But how did that explain the lingering feeling of dread? The sense that someone was coming, that something terrible was about to happen? That someone was watching her? 'Stupid creepy place,' she muttered. 'Imagination.

Definitely. Trick of the light.'

'Amy,' Rory said. 'Nobody's disagreeing with you.'

'Well, good,' she said. 'Quite right, too.'

'Although,' Rory added, 'I don't quite see how the wind blew the lamps alight again.'

The Doctor stopped dead in his tracks. 'I wonder,' he said in exasperation, 'if we could talk a little less. This being an attempt at stealth, remember? And trying not to attract any attention and all the rest of it? Just a suggestion.'

Rory and Amy nodded. The Doctor walked on, and they trailed guiltily behind him. Then he stopped again. 'Ah.'

Amy peered over his shoulder. The doors to the council chamber were round the next bend in the corridor, but two of Beol's knights were standing in front of them. 'Are there guards?' asked Rory in a stage whisper. 'I said there'd be guards.'

Amy put her hand on the Doctor's shoulder. 'Right, what's the plan?'

'Plan?'

'I bet it's brilliant.'

'Brilliant.'

'I bet it's so brilliant I could see my own face in it.'

Behind them, Rory said, 'We could always try the side entrance.'

The Doctor and Amy, turning to look at him, said in unison, '*What* side entrance?'

Rory shoved his hands in his pockets and stared down at his feet. 'There's usually one, isn't there? I think I saw some people leave that way earlier... I was sitting over on the side, yes? Not everyone went out of the main doors... Look, it was "just a suggestion"!'

Roughly five and a half minutes later, the three of them came to a halt before an unprepossessing and unguarded door. The Doctor tried the handle. It opened without creaking. 'And we're in!' he said softly and gleefully. He slipped inside, Amy and Rory following close behind, and the travellers found themselves in the arcade that ran around the perimeter of the council chamber.

The hall itself was dark and deserted. Everything was in shadow which only an hour or two earlier had been so full and busy. Up on the dais, two lamps burned behind the throne. The dragon glowed palely. The Doctor made straight for it. He knelt down in front of it and patted it on the snout.

'Don't worry,' he said to it, aiming the sonic screwdriver into its half-open eye. 'This won't hurt.'

The beast shuddered. 'Whoa! Down boy!' The Doctor switched off the sonic, moved round to the side of the dragon and then – gently, ever so gently – used it again to remove a tiny piece of metal from the dragon's side. 'Come here, both of you,' he said to Amy and Rory. 'Come and take a closer look at raw Enamour.'

It was only a scrap – a tiny scale – nestling in the palm of the Doctor's hand. But it was so smooth, and its colour so pure and unusual... Even a piece as small as this, Amy thought, you'd love to have it. You'd love to take it out to look at it and hold it and know that you owned it. You'd love to be able to call it yours...

'You're thinking that it's beautiful, aren't you?' said the Doctor. 'That it's the most gorgeous thing you've ever seen. Rory doesn't match up. Amy doesn't compare. You're wondering what it would be like to have it, you're wondering how you ever lived without it, and you can't understand why anyone would say that it's dangerous. How can anything so gorgeous be so dangerous? But it's all these things – beautiful and necessary and dangerous. The people who made it understood how powerful it was. That's why they called it Enamour. Because it bewitches people. It can turn minds, sell merchandise, sway elections. And it does its job far too well.' The Doctor closed his hand.

Amy drew in a shivery breath. She glanced at

Rory. He looked shaken too. He reached over to take her hand and she held his back, tight.

The Doctor threw the piece up into the air and caught it; once again it shone in his palm. He closed his hand once more – when he opened it, the tiny powerful scrap had disappeared. 'Yes. So that's Enamour,' he said. 'And the thing is, that it was all right wanting it, and getting it, and even wanting more of it – but it didn't stop there. Oh no. There were other effects too, side effects, that nobody predicted. You've felt it already, both of you, haven't you – a necklace here, a spoon there—'

'Or a fork?' Amy suggested.

'Yes, what is it about forks? And the next thing you know, you've gone and put it in your pocket. But then you start thinking – well, is that what people are doing to my stuff? Is that what they're doing with my spoons?'

'Or forks,' Amy said, pointedly.

'Or, as you rightly say, forks. Do you have designs on my forks?' He shot her a fierce look. Amy almost took a step back but then he grinned at her. 'So first you get protective, and then you get suspicious, and the next thing you know you're keeping secrets, and you're getting afraid, and you're wondering if maybe those people you used to call your neighbours aren't quite as friendly as you thought they were. Because look at your amazing stuff! It's so beautiful and necessary – they must want it as much as you do. They must have their eye on it...' He looked around the chamber, into the shadows. Again, Amy had that sense of dread, that something was close, something was watching...

'I think that's been happening here,' Rory said slowly.

'Me too,' said the Doctor. His gaze came to rest on Amy. She let go of Rory's hand and folded her arms. There hadn't been anything. Just a trick of the light.

'I got talking to this old woman earlier,' Rory said suddenly. 'Her name's Hilthe. She used to be on their council here, or whatever it was called, and then Beol rolled up with the Teller and the dragon, and they challenged her in an election, and she lost. It was nothing like the Teller's version of events.' He took out the tile that Hilthe had given him and handed it to the Doctor. His words came more and more rapidly, as if now he'd started to talk he wanted to get it all out. 'She gave me this – I don't know what it is – said that if I wanted to come and hear more about the good old days I should come and visit her. I don't think this Enamour stuff affects her, Doctor. She wasn't wearing any gold, and she couldn't understand why everyone was so... Well, *enchanted* by Beol.'

The Doctor examined the tile closely, studying the marks engraved upon. He flipped it over to look at the back and traced his fingertip along the delicate filigree he found there. 'It's a map of part of the city. I think the black dot on it here is probably your friend's house. This is her calling card.' He threw it back over to Rory. 'Hilthe. She sounds like somebody we should get to know better. Think you could persuade her to come and talk to me?'

'I'll give it a go.' Rory turned to Amy. 'Coming?'

She shook her head. 'No, I'll stay here. I want to find out more about this metal stuff. Where it came from. How it got here. Why there's so much of it. I'll see you in the rooms later.'

'Where it came from,' the Doctor repeated, as Rory went on his way. 'How it got here. Why there's so much of it. Anything else you'd like, while I'm at it?'

'Cup of tea would be nice, thanks, but dragon facts will do for now.'

'Right.' The Doctor flipped out the sonic screwdriver again. 'Well, the reason there's so much, is that working with the metal makes more of it. The more you do to it, the more there is of it. Like instant coffee.'

'I'd rather that cup of tea,' Amy said. 'But that's why it oozes and wriggles and gets everywhere?'

'That's why.'

'So how about where it came from and how it got here?'

'Let's see what we can find out...' Sonic screwdriver in hand, the Doctor wandered around the dragon. It didn't move but, watching it lie there, its eye half-open, Amy couldn't quite shake the feeling that it was only biding its time, waiting to stir and rise up from the dais...

'It won't move, you know,' the Doctor said. He was on the left side of the dragon, and was apparently trying to prise it open. 'Not unless I tell it to move.' He thought about what he had just said. 'Or the people who made it turn up again and tell it to move.'

'Is that likely to happen?'

'I don't think so—'

'You don't *think* so?'

'That's the best I can manage until I find out something about the provenance of this beastie... Oh, here we are!'

He had managed to loosen a section of the dragon; a piece of metal much larger than the single scale he had detached before. This was the size of a dinner plate, thinner and slightly curved. The Doctor turned it over several times to study it and then he handed it over to Amy. 'As I said. Not likely to happen.'

When Amy examined it, she saw marks engraved on it. Letters, presumably. 'Doctor, not all of us are fluent in technobabble.'

'No? What do they teach you in those schools?' He took the panel back. 'Manufacturer's details. Like a hallmark. And what that tells me, Amy, is that our big old friendly worm here was made a very long time ago, by a civilisation that was out travelling between the stars before life even put in an appearance on this world.' He stared intently down at the metal, as if he might somehow catch sight of that distant, ancient species and learn something about them. 'Think about it. This was an empty world back then. No people. Leaving the dragon here was like burying your treasure under a tree in the corner of a quiet field. But that was aeons ago. I doubt its owners will be back for it. In the meantime, it's not doing anybody here any good. We need to get rid of it.'

He put the panel back into place and used the sonic screwdriver to reattach it. Amy walked slowly round the dragon, admiring the curves of its wings, the long sweep of its tail. Knowing that it was so old, so alien, made it even more fascinating. 'I wonder what made them leave it here. Why would you do that? It's so...'

'Go on,' said the Doctor. 'It's so...?'

'So beautiful,' Amy said honestly. 'I think it's

the most beautiful thing I've ever seen.'

'It isn't, though. It's only making you think that it is.' He pulled a face. 'Although, having seen Leadworth, this could well be the most beautiful thing you've ever seen. But mostly what you're feeling is the effect of Enamour. When it wears off, this will be—'

'A completely ordinary big gold dragon of uncertain alien provenance.'

The Doctor grinned at her. 'Precisely that.'

'So why abandon it? If it's so special to them? Why give it up?'

'Why does anyone bury their treasure? Perhaps they were in trouble and they couldn't carry it with them. Trying to escape trouble. Big universe, plenty of trouble.'

'A war? An invasion?'

'That's the kind of thing. Or maybe they stole it and hid it so that they weren't caught with it when the bill turned up.'

Amy began to laugh. 'A heist gone wrong!'

'Maybe! Why not? Jewel theft, Amy,' he said grandly, 'is a universal constant. But chances are we'll never find out the full story.' He leaned his elbow on the beast casually, almost too casually. Amy gave him a questioning frown. He raised an eyebrow and jerked his head slightly, gesturing behind him. Someone there, Amy guessed, listening to them talk. How much had they heard? 'But there are a few things we could learn,' the Doctor went on. 'Very easily.'

'Oh yes?' Amy kept her tone light.

'Yes.' He draped one arm proprietarily over the dragon. 'Such as – where did Beol and the Teller find the dragon? Who were they before they turned up here in Geath? How did they find out how to make it work for them? And are they anything more than a couple of conmen?' Without turning his head, the Doctor called back over his shoulder. 'So why don't you stop lurking in the shadows like a bad stage villain, come out here, and start telling the truth rather than spinning a pack of lies?'

Chapter

4

'**A chord**,' **Rory said** with confidence, as he walked along the empty criss-cross streets of Geath, 'is the line between two points on a curve.' Truly, as the Doctor had promised, the universe was full of marvels. Here, on an alien world in a strange city under the spell of a mysterious substance not entirely within his comprehension, Rory had finally found a use for GCSE maths. Without it (and Hilthe's map, to be fair) he would be literally walking round in circles.

'You'll find a use for it one day, Williams,' Rory muttered, in a passable imitation of Mr Swallow, Head of Maths, which would have made Amy laugh, if Amy hadn't been half a mile away and behaving weirdly. More weirdly. Even more weirdly than running away with a charismatically chaotic time traveller the night before her wedding. *Their* wedding. That was already weird enough for Rory. And yet still he found himself picking his way round said strange city in the middle of the night in search of a little old lady. And why? Because the Doctor had asked him to. Talk about Enamour. 'So if I go up these steps… and along this alley… then I should come out—'

Into another plaza, this one as deserted as the rest of the city, the tinkling water in its fountain the only sound to be heard. The buildings glistered eerily under the moon. 'Weird weird *weird*. It is all too weird. I don't like it.' Rory examined the tile that Hilthe had given him and turned ninety degrees anticlockwise. He headed down a broad avenue lined with trees tottering under the weight of the decorations loaded onto them.

Hilthe's house, when he found it, stood out a mile – it was the only one not slathered in Enamour. Rory ran up the steps and pulled on the bell. As he waited, he studied the stained glass on the nearest window. Even in the dim light, its vibrant colours and intricate design gave a clue to how Geath must have looked before the metal had oozed out of the council chamber and coated everything, turning the city uniform.

A servant answered the door. Rory showed him the tile and was led into a sitting room that was warm, comfortable, and conspicuously gold-free. As he waited, Rory looked at some of the pictures: paintings and sketches of Geath throughout its long history. On the shelves and in the cabinets were other treasures: badges of office, old books and documents, portraits of the long-dead great and good. So many people, so many of the symbols and artefacts that must have meant so much to them over the years. Hilthe, Rory understood properly now, was an important part of that history, and this room was a shrine to it. What had the Doctor said? Twelve and a half thousand years. What would it be like, to have that much weight of the past behind you? How would it feel, knowing that you had failed to persuade your fellow citizens that all those years of tradition were worth keeping? That the long chain of history was ending with you?

Hilthe arrived, wearing a crimson quilted dressing gown and showing no outward sign of minding that she had been woken up in the middle of the night by a near stranger. The famous Geathian hospitality at last. She sat them down by the hearth, and her servant poured glasses of a hot, sweet tea, while Rory explained in the simplest terms possible what it was that they had discovered so far.

'The friend I'm travelling with, the Doctor – he's taken a closer look at the metal that the dragon's made from, and it's worried him.' He took a sip. 'Anyway, the Doctor thinks it might be having some sort of *effect* on the people of the city.' He sipped again, marshalling his thoughts. 'And that might be why the Teller and Beol have been able to control them. The metal kind of makes people believe what the Teller says.'

'A metal that can change minds?' Hilthe frowned. 'That doesn't sound very likely.'

'I know it sounds… well, weird, but it's the truth. I've seen it happen. We only arrived in the city this evening, and Amy's already been affected.'

'Amy?'

'My other friend. My girlfriend. We heard noises in the council complex and went to investigate. Awful noises – screeching, shrieking. Amy ran off ahead, but when we caught up with her, she hardly seemed to know what we were talking about. I think the metal – Enamour, it's called – makes people forget things, or suppress them, or keep them secret.'

Hilthe sat back in her chair. She studied Rory carefully. 'Strange metals, strange noises – all told, this is a very strange tale.'

'But true. Honestly. If you come and meet the Doctor, he'll explain, better than I can. He's good at making the outright bizarre sound completely reasonable.'

'Not necessarily a quality. But can he help? Can he help Geath?'

'Help is what the Doctor does. Help is what the Doctor *is*.'

Hilthe sat in silent contemplation for a while, studying the different treasures that lined the walls of her home. Then, apropos of nothing, she said, 'When do you and Amy marry?'

'In the morning… How did you know we were getting married?'

Hilthe nodded at his hands. 'When you started talking about her, you began playing with that wedding band.'

'What?' Rory looked down. Sure enough, he was fiddling with a gold ring. Where had that come from? He didn't remember picking it up. It sat in the centre of his palm. 'Hilthe, this isn't mine.' As he spoke, the ring suddenly twisted round of its own accord. He tried to drop it, but it seemed to him that it writhed in his hand, refusing to be let go. 'I can't stop it!'

Hilthe got out of her seat and leaned over to still his hands. Gently but firmly, she took the ring from him. She held it up in front of her to examine it more closely, and Rory caught a glimpse of her sharp, clever eye through it. Then Hilthe blinked.

She shuddered and doubled over, giving a small cry of pain.

Rory jumped out of his seat and ran to help her but, before he could get close enough, he bounced back. He stretched out his hands. They came up against something solid. Rory pushed hard against it, desperate to get to the old woman, who was now shaking violently.

'Hilthe!' he cried, thumping against the barrier between them.

But there was no way through, no matter how hard he hit or pushed. Rory pressed his hands against the invisible barrier and watched helplessly as pulsing golden light began to emanate from the ring. Small circles at first, expanding rapidly until Hilthe was entirely enveloped by the light. Her skin became translucent, as if she was made of clear crystal that was lit from within. The ring, cupped in her hands, began to glow. Her head was bowed and Rory could not see her face.

'Hilthe,' Rory whispered in awe. 'Are you still in there? Can you speak to me?'

Hilthe raised her head and opened her eyes. White fire. She looked like an angel... Rory dismissed the idea at once as ridiculous. No such thing. Aliens, however...

'Who are you? What do you want?'

The voice that answered was like Hilthe's, but

richer and sweetened with a hundred thousand harmonies. Rory was reminded of the Teller earlier – but his voice sounded shrill and harsh in comparison.

'I am the Herald. I speak for my masters, the Bright Nobles of the Feond. I have come to claim what is rightfully theirs.' Her glance darted to and fro, searching, or hunting. She repeated her greeting. 'I am the Herald. I speak for my masters, the Bright Nobles of the Feond. I have come to claim what is rightfully theirs.' Her eyes caught him. 'We can reward you well.'

It wasn't exactly hard to guess what she was talking about. Rory knew that the Doctor thought Geath should be rid of it, that Hilthe wanted Geath to be rid of it… and yet, and yet the city was so beautiful now… Without the gold, it would look so bare, so dull, hardly anything at all…

'There's nothing here,' Rory said. 'Look around you. Sorry. Try the next planet along.'

The Herald took in her surroundings – and saw only Hilthe's ungilded sitting room. Then she sighed, a full chord that resonated with grief and loss. A wave of guilt washed over Rory, but the truth stuck to his tongue. The light went out. Hilthe staggered backwards. Rory grabbed her arm to stop her falling and guided her back to her chair.

She sat for a few moments with her head bowed. 'How strange. How strange.' Then she sat up, as if she had come to a decision. 'I want to meet your Doctor friend.' She paused. 'I'm not sure why you just lied. No, don't deny it. But he will certainly need to know what you've seen in my house. My view of it was... difficult to describe, so you're going to have to tell the Doctor everything. If he's going to help me.' She gave Rory a very sharp look. 'And I mean everything.'

The Teller emerged from the shadow of the arcade. Two knights followed close behind him, their hands resting lightly on the hilts of their sheathed short swords. 'Well,' said the Teller affably, 'here is a curious thing. The last I saw of our guests from Dant, they were being shown to their very fine quarters. And yet barely a bell has rung and here they are in the council chamber. Whatever could have brought them here?'

'We're not from Dant,' the Doctor said. 'But you know that already.'

The Teller walked over to the dragon, placing one hand upon its head and the other upon the highest point of one folded wing. It was about as deliberate a display of possession as it was possible to make.

The Doctor ran one finger along the dragon's

tail. 'Go on,' he said. 'Tell me where you found it. I bet it makes a brilliant story.'

The Teller lifted a hand – one only. 'But my friend! You have already heard a great story this evening!'

'Not a true one, though.'

'Does a story have to be true to be great?'

'It helps.'

'But what more does my tale require?' The Teller stroked the dragon's head. Beneath his touch, the metal began to glisten.

And then, Amy would swear, it began to sing. A low sweet sound just on the edge of her hearing that picked up and harmonised with the Teller's voice. She shivered. Where had she heard that before?

The Teller talked on. 'My tale has excitement and adventure and – most of all – it has an *enemy*. That was what the people of Geath wanted to hear. This city!' He sneered. 'Year upon year of comfortable talk, always the same, always too safe – in their hearts they *longed* for something new. Something dangerous. So that is what I give them. And when they become too afraid, I can remind them that even if there are powers in this world that threaten them, Beol is here. Beol will protect them.' He gave a crooked smile. 'And that is no more than the truth. Beol is a good king.'

'There shouldn't be a king. Not here.'

The Teller's smile turned radiant. 'But now there is. And how they love him!'

'Were you a storyteller before?' The Doctor's voice, which until now had sounded faint in comparison, became steadily more authoritative, more natural – more *real*. 'Were they good stories?' He walked slowly around the dragon. The Teller didn't budge an inch, but monitored his adversary's progress closely. 'Did they tell people how to live their lives just that bit better? Did they inspire them? Inform them? Entertain them? Or were they rubbish? Were they hack work? Was there always a good guy and a bad guy and a tidy resolution at the end? Have you simply found a way to amplify your voice so that people can't help listening?'

The Teller's hitherto genial air was gone. He gripped the dragon's head. Beneath his hands, the golden hide began to ripple.

'Doctor,' Amy murmured. 'I think you're making him angry.' She glanced uneasily at the shifting metal. 'I think you're making it angry.'

'You have no right to be here,' the Teller said harshly. 'I should have you put in the stocks. You're a fool!'

'And you're a liar. Can't bear to hear the truth? Can't bear to hear it said?' Subtly, the Doctor's voice began to change again. Now it was in tune with the dragon.

The hum was louder than ever before. Amy pressed her fingers against her ears. The dragon-song was swelling. 'Doctor, I don't think this is a good idea—'

'But you know it in your heart, don't you?' the Doctor said, ignoring her. 'It's the dragon that makes them listen. It's Beol that they love.'

'Stop this! Stop this at once!'

Amy looked across the hall. An old woman was striding towards them, her eyes flashing in anger. Rory came hurrying behind her. This must be his friend Hilthe.

'This is the council chamber of Geath, the Heart of the City!' Hilthe said. 'Generation after generation of our people have gathered here in comradeship and concord. Show some respect to their efforts, to their memory!' She turned to Rory. 'Is this your friend?'

Rory nodded. 'This is the Doctor.'

The Doctor stepped back from the dragon. He bowed his head. 'Forgive me, Mother, I meant no disrespect.'

She gave him an unfavourable look and turned to address the Teller. 'I know you hold this city in contempt—'

'Not true, Mother!' the Teller said quickly; too quickly, Amy thought.

The Doctor murmured, 'The Teller doth protest too much... Now why would that be, I wonder...?'

Hilthe held up her hand to stop the Teller speaking further. 'But you might at least make a show of respect. Given that making a show is all you're good for. Now,' she turned back to address the Doctor. 'Your friend has come to me with a most remarkable tale, one which any sensible person would hardly find credible. What truth is there in it? What does it mean for my city and its people?'

The Doctor held up his hands. 'I'd like to tell you, Mother, but you arrived just as our friend here was having me thrown into the stocks.' He gave the Teller his madman's grin. 'Which is it to be? Throw me out or hear me out? Because I can tell you a story that will turn your world upside down. You know I can. And this story will be wonderful and terrible and brilliant – and it won't need a villain.'

Amy could see that the Teller was torn between his need to rid himself of the Doctor and his desire to find out more from him. He vacillated for a moment or two, and then turned to the two guards and dismissed them. 'Go on,' he said to the Doctor. 'Impress me.'

'Good man! Good choice!'

Rory came to stand next to Amy. 'Did we nearly find ourselves in the stocks?'

'Nearly. But not actually. And, you know, in a case like that it really isn't the thought that counts.'

'Hm.' Rory was not mollified.

The Doctor rubbed his hands together, cracked some knuckles, and then turned the sonic screwdriver onto the dragon.

The Teller made an anxious movement towards him. 'Don't damage it!'

'I won't damage it! Well, not so as you'd notice... Ah, here we go! Come and take a look at this, both of you.'

It was another dragon-scale. Hilthe raised her eyebrows at Rory, who nodded encouragingly, and she stepped towards the Doctor. The Teller came to look, too, and, as he stared down at the scrap of Enamour lying in the Doctor's palm, his face changed. Everything distinctive about him – his wit, his intelligence – leached away. He became absent. Amy shivered. Was that how she and Rory had looked? From the moment she had picked up the dragon-hammer on the gate and resented the Doctor touching it, the metal had been working on them.

The Doctor, watching the Teller, nodded. 'I thought that you hadn't been on the receiving end before. Feels different, this way round, doesn't it?'

'I feel nothing,' Hilthe said. 'What is this? Some kind of conjuring trick?'

The Doctor closed his hand.

The Teller shuddered and pulled back. 'No, something definitely happened then.' He looked at the Doctor with new respect – and then at the dragon, with new apprehension.

'I don't know where you found it,' the Doctor said. 'I wonder if you could tell me even if you wanted to. Enamour – that's its name – it makes people possessive, jealous. Makes them keep secrets.' He glanced at Amy and gave her a rueful look. 'Even from people they can trust. Right, Amy?'

'Oh,' Amy said. 'I know. I guess there was… something… sort of. Maybe.' She tried to speak, but the words wouldn't form. 'Why can't I say what it was?'

'Amy…' The Doctor pressed two long fingers gently against her cheek. 'It's not your fault – it's what Enamour does. There's no harm done. But try to concentrate now. Try to tell me what it was you saw in the dark. Was it big? Was it scary? Animal? Vegetable? Mineral? Accidental?'

Amy struggled to get past the mist descending around her and to ignore the gentle lulling hum rising steadily inside her head. 'It was big… No, not at first. It grew. It got bigger and bigger. All the lamps went out – it made them go out. There was a howling sound. Well, you heard that. It sort of came towards me. I thought it was going to attack me!' Rory took hold of her hand. 'Then it stopped. It loomed for a while. It made me feel afraid, and alone. Then it went away. I put my hand through it, and it just went away. Like it wasn't really there.'

Through the haze, the Doctor was smiling at her; approvingly, encouragingly. Another memory came back, in a flash. 'Doctor, I think people were whispering about it earlier, in the chamber. They've seen it here before!' It was, as Rory was no doubt thinking, weird. As if, knowing that it was real for others, she was suddenly able to admit its existence to herself. The humming was quieter, and the Doctor was frowning, thoughtfully. 'Go on, tell us,' Amy said. 'What is it?'

'A scout, probably. Trying to find the metal. Question now – is it an automatic manifestation, or is there someone behind it? Has somebody sent it? Because if they have, our sleeping dragon over there might not be quite as quiescent as we'd like.'

The Teller looked anxiously at the dragon. 'Is it dangerous?'

'Dangerous?' Hilthe turned to the Doctor. 'Is it? What does this mean for the city?'

'The dragon alone is danger enough,' the Doctor

said, looking pointedly at the Teller, who looked away guiltily. 'But… if it's automatic, no. And if there's someone behind it…' The Doctor thought for a moment. 'They'll follow the old protocols. They'll send a Herald to ask for the return of the metal before they try to take it by force.'

'Ah,' said Rory, quietly. 'I think we may already have seen that.'

The Doctor gave him a 'you-took-your-time' look. 'Did it ask for its Enamour back?'

'Yes, but – Doctor, I said there wasn't any here! I couldn't stop myself!'

'Oh dear.'

'I couldn't!'

Hilthe interrupted. 'It's all right, Rory.' She looked at the Doctor. 'I should imagine the Doctor will tell us that it is the work of this metal again.'

'But… if they take it by force—'

Hilthe laid her hand upon Rory's shoulder. 'I'm sure that we will be given another chance before any assault is made upon us.' She reached into her pocket and held out the ring for the Doctor to see. 'This is the means by which their messenger spoke to me, Doctor. Do not ask me how. I believe, however, that I could understand a little of her mind.'

The Doctor peered at the ring. 'May I?'

'Of course.'

The Doctor picked up the ring. He held it up to the light – his eye, dark and intelligent, was briefly visible through it – and then he tested it with the sonic screwdriver. 'Definitely the same material. You say it spoke to you?'

'*Through* me would be nearer the mark.'

'So it could still be an automatic system…'

'Automatic,' the Teller said. 'You keep saying that. But what does it mean?'

'Ooh, good one. Not easy to explain. Let's see what you make of this. Imagine, if you can, machines that don't need people to operate them. Machines that can be told in advance what to do, and then left to get on with it.' He grinned at the Teller, whose eyes widened as the idea sank in. 'You *are* imagining it, aren't you? Good for you!'

'Doctor,' Hilthe said, 'I have a question. Why does this material… What did you call it?'

'Enamour.'

'*Enamour.*' She experimented with the word. 'Why does it not affect me, when the rest of the city is enthralled?'

The Doctor shrugged. 'Wisdom? You've seen it all before?'

Hilthe laughed. 'You mean I'm old!'

'Why are *you* not affected?' the Teller asked the Doctor.

The Doctor winked at him. 'Same reason.'

The Teller stared at him, fascinated and bewildered, like he was watching a magician whose tricks he could not understand.

'Now,' said Hilthe briskly, returning to the business at hand, 'tell me if I have misunderstood, but as I see it, what we ought to do now is determine whether the makers of this dragon are indeed trying to speak to us, or whether an echo of their voice has in some way travelled down the long years to us.'

'I'm impressed!' said the Doctor. 'You're impressive!'

'Thank you, Doctor, I know that already. Now, given that I am in some way impervious to this metal's deleterious effects, surely what I ought to do next is try this ring once again in order to summon its makers?'

'Too dangerous, Doctor,' Rory said, quickly. 'Anything might happen.'

The Doctor frowned. 'He's right, Mother—'

'Nevertheless, the decision is mine and mine alone,' Hilthe took the ring back from him. 'Besides, for the city of Geath, I would do anything.'

Chapter
5

Hilthe cupped the ring in her hands and was bathed once again in the rings of golden light. Amy was amazed. 'It's beautiful! Is that what happened before?'

'Just wait till she starts speaking.' Rory felt his stomach knotting with anticipation. Somehow, the fear he had felt for Hilthe dissipated, and he was eager for Amy to see what he had seen, and anxious to see it again himself.

When the Herald returned, the show was even more impressive than he remembered. The light was more intense, the experience more involving, more complete. The Herald's voice rang around the high chamber like a peal of bells. 'I am the Herald. I speak for my masters, the Bright Nobles of the

Feond. I have come to claim what is rightfully theirs.'

The Doctor walked slowly all the way round the apparition, fascinated, his head tilted to one side as he studied her. 'You're amazing. And you're here, aren't you? Well, not *here* here, because this is a transmission. But it isn't a recording. You're not a voice from the past. You're speaking to us now, aren't you?'

The Herald turned her head to follow the Doctor as he moved, watching him with her fire-lit eyes. 'I am speaking to you now,' she confirmed. 'I am speaking to you for my masters, the Bright Nobles of the Feond. I have come to claim what is rightfully theirs. Who is the Noble here? Who has authority to speak?'

The Teller took a step forwards, but the Doctor got in first. 'You can speak to me. Where have you come from?'

'I am the Herald. I speak for my masters, the Bright Nobles of the Feond. I have come to claim what is rightfully theirs.'

'Yes, I've got that already. You want your treasure and I have to say I'll be glad to see the back of it. So will the people of Geath. Not at first, probably.' The Doctor glanced quickly at the Teller. 'When I say "probably", I mean "definitely". Let's not worry about that right now. Why should I hand it over?'

'It belongs to my masters, the Bright Nobles of the Feond. It is rightfully theirs.'

'Yes, yes, so you say. But my problem with that is anyone can turn up and claim that old Smaug over there belongs to them.' The Doctor looked at the Teller again, pointedly this time. 'I'll admit that the light show is impressive – very whizz bang – but it's not proof of purchase, is it? So why should I hand it over to you?'

The Herald closed her eyes briefly, as if calculating, or perhaps receiving instructions. 'We can reward you well.'

'Oops,' said Amy. 'Bad move.'

The Doctor bared his teeth in a mirthless smile. He strolled around the Herald one more time, coming to a halt slightly behind her left side. He put his hand flat against the sphere of light. It rippled almost imperceptibly but otherwise did not change. 'Problem is,' he said, drawing back his hand and examining his palm, 'Enamour is a banned substance. Banned by everyone. You name them, they've banned it. Outlawed within the Ancient Bounds of the League of Perpetual Accord. Forbidden on every count across the Uncounted Constellations. The Hieromonks of the Hexagon preach against it from every pulpit in the Church of All the Levels, and the Bloodied Mercenaries of

Metis IV ("may-their-name-be-accursed-through-the-universe") wouldn't touch it, even if you paid them. Which you have to. So why should you get it?'

'It belongs to my masters. When it is restored to them, they will treat it with care. They treat all that they own with care.'

'Oh, yes, you say that now! But dumping it here on Geath was hardly careful, was it? Talk about toxic waste! It's been making a right old mess of things around here! Fine republican tradition, twelve thousand years plus or minus, throw some Enamour at them and the next thing you know they're going all moon-faced over a king. A *king* of all things! And, to be fair, he's a nice chap, good shoulders, I'm sure he makes a very good king – *but*,' the Doctor paused for breath and raised a reproving finger, 'where would we be without tradition?'

The light around the Herald began to grow in intensity. Urgently, she said, 'It belongs to my masters—'

'You do go on about your masters, did you know that? Anyone might suspect them of using a mind-controlling metal to make you go all wobbly. Anyway, they're not my masters. I can take care of the stuff. I shall take care of the stuff. Won't hand it over. Shan't.'

'They are coming!' cried the Herald.

The light was now dazzling. Amy had to shield her eyes. Rory and the Teller did the same. Amy heard the Teller whispering to himself, *'What is this? What is this?'* She put her hand on his shoulder. 'Don't worry. The Doctor will sort it all out. Definitely. Probably.'

'Our enemies are close!' cried the Herald. 'They must not take it!'

'Enemies?' The Doctor came round to face her. 'Oh, now we're onto something. What enemies?'

'There was a war,' said the Herald.

'Oh, there usually is.'

'We lost. We lost our beloved worlds! A hundred thousand worlds, lost to us! We hid all that we could rather than let it fall into the hands of the enemies. They would not use it for peace; for beauty.'

'Said it was a war,' said Amy.

'*I* said it was a war,' replied the Doctor. '*You* said it was a heist.'

'We became exiles.' The Herald's beautiful voice had turned piteous.

'I said it *might* be a heist,' Amy muttered.

'Nothing wrong with a spot of exile,' the Doctor said to the Herald. 'Not a bad way of life. See the sights, move on, see a few more sights—'

'Save the odd Star Whale,' said Amy.

'Fight the odd vampire,' said Rory.

The Doctor turned on them. 'Technically speaking, they weren't vampires... Do I look like Buffy?' He nodded towards the Herald. 'Can I get on with talking to the bright shiny potential alien menace, please? Herald, what happened?'

'Our home was lost to us. We wandered for so long that we could barely remember what we had once owned. We wandered through the dark and the cold. We could barely remember our worlds, our homes. We began to forget the light and the music and the bliss.'

Amy bit her lip and looked at the Doctor. No more banter from him, no more questions. He looked old, very old, unspeakably sad, and alone. What was it the Teller had said earlier? That he only told the people of Geath what they wanted to hear... 'Doctor,' she said, 'you reckoned that the dragon must have been here for millennia. So why now? What's brought them here now?'

'We heard an echo from the past,' the Herald said. 'It called to us. We came.'

The Doctor brought himself back to the present. 'It was probably when the Geathians started working the metal.' His voice was more subdued than before. 'That must have triggered something – a beacon, perhaps. Enough for the Herald's people to work out where the dragon was – and for their enemies to work it out, too. Whoever they are.'

The Herald quivered at the mention of them. 'They are very close! They are coming! Do not let them take it from us!'

'Doctor,' Rory said. 'Wouldn't it be best just to let them take it? Away from here. Before those things Amy saw come for us.'

'No!' Amy said quickly. 'How do we know that they're telling us the truth? They could be spinning us a story.' She glanced at the Teller. 'Like everyone else round here.'

'We have to get rid of the stuff somehow,' Rory said. 'It can't stay here in Geath. So why not save ourselves a job and send it back where it came from?'

'Rory, you never listen!'

'*Me* never listen? That's rich coming from you, Amy Pond!'

'Oh, *now* we're getting to the truth of things!'

'Amy, this isn't actually about you. Don't you get it? Look at Hilthe. I'm worried about her! How long are we going to leave her like this? She's an old woman—'

The Doctor spoke over them, addressing the Herald in a gentler voice. 'Tell me about your enemies.'

The light around the Herald dimmed, as if it was being pulled away from her. 'They brought chaos. They brought ruin. My masters were artists and poets and philosophers. Our cities shone like beacons. Our worlds were paradises. But they were destroyed.'

'Why?' pressed the Doctor. 'Why you? Why would anyone do that to you?'

'*Envy*.' Her voice hit a low note that tolled around the hall. 'Jealousy. What other force could tear down towers, shred the learning of ages, consign the Bright Nobles to darkness?' She held her hand out to him, like a beggar pleading for aid. 'We have so little left! Do not let them take it!' The light within her dimmed perilously low. 'They are coming! They have found us! They are here!'

Amy heard once again the low wail that she had chased through the complex earlier. As the sound grew louder, her sense of dread got steadily worse, until she felt sick. What was doing this, Amy thought desperately, as she shoved her fingers into her ears. Travelling with the Doctor, she was often scared, but something about this noise got inside her and made her want to curl up and disappear, like the lamp she had been carrying earlier. 'Doctor!' she yelled. 'Bad guy! Incoming!'

At the far end of the chamber, behind the throne, darkness began to take shape and form, coalescing into a figure. The light around the Herald flickered madly and her body went into spasm.

'Hilthe!' Rory shouted. He tried to reach the old woman, but could not get close. When Amy went to pull him back he shook her off.

The Teller stood with his mouth hanging open, his expression partly of terror, partly of wonder.

'Get back!' Amy yelled at him. 'Let the Doctor handle it!'

Coming to his senses, the Teller rushed to take cover behind one of the columns of the arcade. Amy and Rory joined him. The Doctor remained by the Herald. He stood staring in delight at the figure emerging at the far side of the hall.

It was growing rapidly in size. Now it was Amy's height, now taller, now more than twice the size of an average human, its limbs lengthening, unfurling like wings. Soon it was almost touching the dome of the council chamber and it didn't stop growing. No longer able to fit, it stooped forwards, a huge shadow looming over them all. The noise it was making, amplified by the dome of the chamber, was almost unbearable. And then, through the din, Amy heard a steady hum, very low at first, but getting louder. Harmonies were added to it until it was as if a thousand voices, in perfect unison, were countering the cry of the dark figure across the chamber. Then the Herald, too, began to grow.

Rory grabbed Amy's arm. 'She's fighting back!

Hilthe's fighting back!'

'It's not Hilthe!' Amy shouted, but either he hadn't heard or else it made no difference. Rory whooped and cheered her on.

The Herald seemed to gain strength and stature from his support. Her rate of growth sped up, and soon her bright figure filled her half of the hall. The two unearthly presences hovered for a moment – facing off, considering the nature of the opposition, gearing up to do battle – and then the Herald attacked. Waves of golden light emanated from her in the direction of her enemy. When they hit, the huge dark figure recoiled, and gave a great howl, like a hundred cats screeching in pain and hatred.

'Got it!' yelled Rory. 'Go Hilthe!'

But Amy gasped in dismay – and then puzzled over her reaction. The creature frightened her and its coming and its presence filled her with terror. So why did she not want it hurt? Was it because it hadn't touched her? All it had done so far was look big and loom and wail – but there wasn't a law against that.

The Herald tried to capitalise on her advantage. She raised one light-filled hand and sent more shock waves out towards her enemy. It buckled under the force of the blow, like a tree blasted by a storm, and shrank somewhat in size. But then it started to gather its resources for a counter-attack. The wailing, which had faltered under the Herald's assault, rose up again with renewed vigour and purpose. It stretched out its vast hands, so that the whole council chamber seemed to lie within its grasp. The two lamps behind the throne went out. The only light now came from the Herald, and its pale reflection in the dragon. Amy saw the Doctor taking cover behind it.

'Amy! Rory! Are you all right?' he yelled.

'Fine!' she shouted back. She glanced at the man next to her who was wide-eyed and clutching at the column as if it was the only solid thing in a world turned to chaos. 'Though I think the Teller might need therapy!'

'What about Hilthe?' Rory shouted. 'Doctor, is this hurting her?'

The Doctor didn't get a chance to answer. The Herald's enemy made a grab for her. It was as if it was trying to extinguish her, to snuff her out like she was a candle. The Herald's light diminished again. She gave an agonised shriek – and then her light dissipated entirely. The whole apparition withered, shrank, and then was gone. Only Hilthe remained – a tiny, silver-haired old woman, clutching an innocuous-looking gold ring. She stood still and erect for a moment, as if the shock was enough to keep her upright, and then she slumped to the ground. The ring fell out of her hands. It clattered coldly against the tiled floor, then rolled across the chamber and came to a halt in front of the dragon. The Doctor picked it up and put it in his pocket.

'Hilthe!' Rory cried in dismay. He ran out from the cover of the arcade and helped the Doctor carry her back to one of the seats there. She sat with her head down. Rory put his arm around her. 'Hilthe,' he said gently. 'Can you hear me? Are you all right?'

The Teller, creeping across to stand beside the Doctor, stared in horror at the monster hovering at the far side of the chamber. The noise had lessened considerably and was now nothing more than a background growl, but the figure was still huge. 'What *is* that thing?'

'Like I said before, it's a scout,' the Doctor said. 'It's been sent to track down the Enamour. Bet you're sorry you found that dragon now.'

The Teller was aghast. 'Sent by *whom*?'

'Good question. Don't know. Yet.'

Hilthe, leaning back in the circle of Rory's arms, opened her eyes. 'Ah!' she cried softly.

The Doctor knelt down beside her and took her hand. 'I'm sorry I let you speak for us, Mother.'

She extricated her hand from his. 'You didn't let me. I insisted.' She shivered. 'I saw many wonderful things through its eyes. Many marvels. Such beautiful cities! Such grandeur!' She shook her head, as if to clear it of whatever strange visions the Herald had placed there. 'However, I see that its enemy is still amongst us. We must determine whether it means my city any harm.'

'So we should.' The Doctor looked back over his shoulder. 'It doesn't seem in a hurry to finish us off, does it? I wonder what it has to say for itself.' Leaving Hilthe in Rory's expert and devoted care, he jumped to his feet and ran out from the cover of the arcade. The alien towered over him. 'Hello!' he said. 'Nice to meet you! Now, call me a romantic if you like – and I am *awfully* romantic about meeting new life forms, brings a lump to the throat – but I don't think you're going to hurt us, are you? Not immediately, anyway. Am I right?' As he was speaking, the alien twisted round slowly, and bent forwards to examine the Doctor. Its jaw hinged open, offering a glimpse down a cavernous mouth. 'Or am I wrong?' Now standing nose-to-snout with it, the Doctor gave a little wave. 'Hello again!'

The creature spoke, its voice low and monotone. 'I represent the Regulatory Board. Under Clause 9.4b (subsection 12.2) of the Regulation of Psycho-Manipulatory Metals Act (30673.26), all parties here assembled must hand over any substances covered by said Act within ten standard time units.'

'That was a mouthful. Can you do it again?'

It did.

'So you can. Good for you! Not easy learning lines like that. If you ever decide to get out of the regulatory business, I suggest you think about the stage. So you want the stuff, too.' The Doctor rocked back and forth on his heels. 'Enamour, Enamour, they all want Enamour… So what's your claim? Who's your boss? Not these Bright Nobles, I bet.'

It growled at that name. 'My authority comes from the Reconstruction Oversight Committee—'

'The *what*?' The Doctor clutched his head in pain. 'That's a *rubbish* name! Who sold you that one? You should get your money back… Did nobody talk to you about brand management? And as for "standard time units"…' He groaned. 'That's rubbish too! What were you *thinking*? You know, if you're serious about reconstructing whatever it is you're busy reconstructing, you should probably get rid of that committee.'

With a sudden quick movement, the Doctor stuck his arm right through the Regulator. It all but disappeared. 'Huh,' he said, half to the Regulator, half to himself. 'Definitely a projection. Doesn't stop you being alarming. The trick with the lights is a good one, too, I'll give you that. And somehow you're stimulating fear and apprehension… Don't know how you're doing it – not yet, will eventually – but put it all together and it's an effective bad-guy routine, isn't it? Said you should think about the stage.' He pulled back his hand, and the Regulator coalesced back into its whole shape. 'Ooh. That's interesting. I stick my hand through you and you still don't make a move towards me. Ten standard time units. And then what? What do you do then?'

'Under powers granted to the Regulatory Board by the Regulation of Psycho-Manipulatory Metals Act (30673.26), reasonable force can be used to secure all substances covered by said Act.'

'Reasonable force?' The Doctor frowned. 'I don't like the sound of that. Reasonable force is never actually reasonable, is it?'

The Regulator twitched the many fingers of one hand. The lamps behind the throne burst back into flame. Then it pointed up towards the dome. All of them gathered there – the Doctor, Amy, Rory, Hilthe, the Teller – looked up.

'Save us!' the Teller whispered, when he saw what was passing overhead.

Beyond the golden dome of the chamber, silhouetted like a shadow play, two gigantic shapes were moving slowly across the sky above

Geath. Both were winged and had a long thin tail that stretched out behind each of them. Amy even thought she could see a puff of smoke. 'Oh, you're kidding me,' she said. 'They can't possibly be…'

'But look at them!' said Rory. 'They totally are! They're—'

'Don't say it, Rory Williams!'

'— *dragons*! Dragons, Amy! Instant awesome!'

'How can this be happening?' gasped the Teller. He clutched desperately at Amy's arm.

She nearly felt sorry for him. 'It'll all work out fine,' she said comfortingly. 'Just keep your hands off the glittery stuff in future, OK? Doesn't do anyone any good. Doctor, tell me they're not really dragons.'

'Tell me they are,' begged Rory.

'Sorry to disappoint you, Rory,' the Doctor said. 'But of course they're not dragons.' He put a finger to his lips, signalling to everyone to be quiet. 'Listen. What can you hear?'

Amy had to strain to pick out what he meant, because the city was already awakening to this new threat. There were shouts from outside and then a gong sounded repeatedly. But behind it all, distantly but distinctly, Amy heard not the flap of wings, but a low constant and entirely mechanical *thrum*… 'Engines,' she said to the Doctor. 'I can hear engines. They're spaceships, aren't they?'

'Spot on,' he replied. He looked grim. 'And from the sound of those particular engines, they're not just spaceships—'

Hilthe rose from her seat. 'Doctor, I demand to know the meaning of all this!'

'— they're gunships.'

Chapter
6

The Doctor turned on the Regulator in cold rage. It looked back at him impassively. 'This is a pre-industrial world inhabited by a people known throughout the universe for their *pacifism*,' the Doctor spat, 'and you've sent gunships to deal with them! Is that what you call reasonable force?'

With a cry, the Teller turned and ran back into the cover of the dark arcade. The Doctor nodded to Amy to go after him. 'Over to you, Pond.'

Amy saluted him. 'On the case, Doc.'

'Find out what's happening outside,' the Doctor instructed her. 'Keep close to our friend the spin-doctor. He'll be looking for Beol. I want to know what they say to each other. I want to know who they are and where they found this dragon. And I want you never to call me "Doc" again.'

Amy saluted once more and went in pursuit of the Teller. She almost caught up with him as he hurried through the council complex, half-running, half-stumbling as he tried to get outside as quickly as possible. She had to hold back, using the curves of the corridors to conceal her from his sight.

Eventually he led her to a pair of big wooden doors which he threw open, and tumbled out into the big plaza in which the council building stood. Amy went as far as the doorway and hung back in the shadows. She watched as the Teller looked upwards. His hand covered his mouth. The sky was growing steadily brighter.

The plaza was filled with people. Amy slipped through the door and made her way through the crowd, trying to keep close to the Teller while using the others to shield her from his view. It helped that he wasn't looking round. Nobody was looking round. Everyone was looking up. Someone cried out, and the cry was picked up, soon everyone was shouting: *What is it? Who are they? What does this mean?*

High in the night sky above Geath were two spaceships. Golden spaceships, each winged and with a long tail, made from a metal that looked both supple and resilient. They were the image of the dragon that lay slumbering back in the hall. They passed overhead with a scream of engines that sent many people in the plaza diving to the ground.

Amy looked at the faces around her, ordinary men and women, but with absolutely no frame of reference for what they were seeing now. What must this all look like to them? The sound of the engines grew fainter as the ships headed downriver, but the danger had not passed. They must have turned, because the noise grew steadily louder again. While the people gathered here might not entirely understand what they were seeing, they knew enough to be able to tell that the enemy had not left them. They shouted as they struggled with each other to get to the alcoves, the cellars, the places of shelter.

'What are they? Where have they come from?'

'It's Dant! Who else can it be? The beast in the hall – these creatures look just like it! They've come to claim it back! They're going to kill us!' That, and the steady approach of the dragon-ships, sent the crowd into panic.

'Be quiet!' shouted the Teller. 'Calm down!' His voice rang out above the noise. He could still speak with authority and persuasiveness. People stopped panicking to listen to him. He pointed upwards.

'Dant? How can it be Dant? How could the people of Dant *possibly* have anything like that?'

'Who is it, then? We took the dragon from them! It has to be them! Who else would do this?'

The Teller opened his mouth to reply. 'Now, this should be worth hearing,' Amy muttered. But whatever he was about to say was sucked up in the scream of the engines. The dragon-ships were now directly overhead. Then they opened fire.

In the council chamber, the Regulator had turned the concave space of the dome into a huge screen, onto which it was projecting images of the events happening outside. The Doctor, Rory and Hilthe watched in horror as the two dragon-ships made their first pass over Geath.

'Doctor,' Hilthe said, 'what are these creatures?' She had moderated her tone considerably, presumably having realised that making demands was not the best way to extract answers from this stranger. She got her reward.

'They're not creatures,' the Doctor explained. 'They're ships – vessels that can fly in the air. This is a demonstration of power. The Regulators are trying to show how powerful they are in comparison to your people.' He turned angrily to the Regulator. 'That's right, isn't it? You want to scare them into handing over all the Enamour.'

The Regulator bent its head, as if acknowledging that what the Doctor said was true.

The Doctor stood, hands clenched by his side, and watched helplessly as events unfolded on the dome overhead. The gunships flew over once again. When they reached the far side of the city, they opened fire, sending a barrage of shots down the valley, over the buildings, across the river. The ships banked, turned, and flew past for a third time. Then they fired another volley of purple flame over Geath in the direction of the hills. Some trees caught fire. The picture cut to the streets, where people were running for cover.

'My poor city,' Hilthe whispered.

The Regulator panned around Geath, showing a city in turmoil and distress. Then it spoke again. 'Nobody has been harmed. Yet. This is a warning. All substances covered by the Act must be handed over within ten standard time units.' As it spoke it shrank and, as soon as it reached his height, it addressed the Doctor directly. 'We shall be monitoring your progress.' Then it disappeared.

The council chamber was dim and quiet and the dome was dark. The ships were gone, but outside there was the clamour of chaos and confusion. One by one the lamps around the chamber leapt alight.

'How much time exactly is ten standard time

units?' asked Hilthe in an uncertain voice.

The Doctor didn't answer. He thumped his palm hard against the dragon. 'Bureaucrats!' he spat. 'Is there anything in the universe I detest more than bureaucrats? You can travel from the Dawn of Time to the very end of existence, and there they are – the cockroaches of eternity! Bureaucrats! With their rules and their protocols and their procedures and their unshakeable belief in their own right to enforce all that mumbo-jumbo! And their superior firepower to back up their threats! Well, I've had enough! I'm sick of it!' He stood in the centre of the hall and shouted up at the darkened dome. 'Do you hear me? Sick of it! You want all the Enamour? I should hand it over to the Herald right now!'

'*That*,' said Rory in exasperation, 'is what I've been saying for ages. Why does nobody listen to me?'

As they argued, Hilthe finally lost her temper. 'Quiet! Now!' They stopped. 'I am *not* a stupid old woman, but this is simply too much. Too much to digest, all at once, and who can think while you shout at one another? Either one of you tells me right now what is happening here, or I send for the watch and have you both slung into the stocks. *What* is happening?'

The Doctor swung round and stared at her in alarm.

Rory said, 'Go on then!'

The Doctor pulled a face. 'Not me! She's scary! Anyway, she's your friend.'

'What?' Rory said incredulously. 'This whole thing is your fault!'

'How did you work that one out?'

'*You're* the one with the time machine! *I* was on my stag night!'

'Ah. Fair point.' The Doctor turned to Hilthe and clapped his hands together. 'Right. Are you sitting comfortably?'

She glared. 'Doctor, my city is being destroyed. Do not be glib.'

'Destroyed? Hmmm.' His forehead wrinkled. 'No. No. You're right. I'll try to explain…'

The sky above Geath became quieter and darker until, at last, only the moon glimmered above. The dragon-ships were gone, for the moment at least.

Amy checked herself for damage, found none, and then stood up. She reached down to help a young woman get back to her feet – 'OK? Nothing hurt? OK then!' – and then she looked round for the Teller.

He, along with everyone else, had dived for cover when the dragon-ships opened fire. Now he was kneeling on the ground, his arms wrapped round himself, still staring up at the sky.

'I think they've gone for now,' Amy called out, to reassure people, trusting that the Teller wouldn't recognise her voice. 'Check the person next to you. Make sure they're all right.'

As it turned out, she didn't need to issue instructions; the people around her were already looking after each other. A glimpse of the old Geath, she thought, before this horrible stuff smothered its best instincts.

Nobody went near the Teller. Eventually he struggled back to his feet of his own accord. Someone shouted at him, 'This is your doing!'

The Teller looked up in alarm. Three or four men were moving towards him. 'What have I done?'

'You're the one who brought that dragon here!' one of the men said. 'That's what they want, isn't it? You saw those flying beasts – just like that dragon. You stole it from Dant! They've come to collect it, and they'll take their revenge at the same time!'

'That's right!' another said. 'And what can we do? How can we protect ourselves? Our families?' He gestured round angrily. 'Look at it all! This is what you've brought upon Geath!'

It was about to turn ugly. Amy abandoned her cover and ran forward.

'Leave him be! We've got enough problems without fighting each other!'

Several of the people around her shouted out

their agreement. Three of the men who had been threatening the Teller were pulled away by friends or family; the last one stood for a while, glaring, then shook his head, spat on the ground, and turned away.

The Teller stared at Amy, surprised to see her so near. '*Thank you*,' he mouthed. He looked back up at the sky, shaking his head, as if trying to convince himself that what he had seen had been nothing more than a dream or a nightmare. But it hadn't. It had been real.

'You wanted them to believe they had enemies over the next hill,' Amy said to herself. 'Bet it doesn't seem such a great idea now, does it?'

All of a sudden, the Teller swung round and went off at a great pace across the plaza. Amy continued to walk slowly around the crowd, checking on those who were still weeping, or seemed alone. Quietly, she worked her way amongst the distressed, hoping that the people and the emotion and the darkness would be enough to keep her out of the Teller's sight. He crossed the plaza and ran up some steps. Amy lingered behind a pillar at the bottom, helping a child back to his feet, rubbing his knee where he had grazed it when he had been knocked over, and shooing him back to his mother.

At the top of the high stone staircase, the Teller

paused and looked back down the hill across Geath. Surveying the aftermath, Amy thought. She turned to look back and see what he was seeing. Even without the view that the Teller must have from his higher vantage point, it was obvious that the city was in uproar. But – and this was odd – she couldn't see any actual damage. No burning houses, or tumbled stone, just shocked, terrified people. Some stumbling, some sobbing, and some angry.

A band of citizens was gathering in front of the main doors of the council chamber. A handful of Beol's knights stood uneasily between them and the entrance. A chant went up, like the one Amy had heard only a few hours earlier: *Beol. Beol. Beol.* It didn't sound anywhere near as enthusiastic as before. Again, Amy almost felt sorry for the Teller, at how quickly his rule through Beol was falling apart – but he did have nobody but himself to blame.

Lost in this vision of chaos and terror, it was almost too late when she heard footsteps running back down the steps. Amy pressed back into the shadows and the Teller hurried past. He had raised his hood to cover his face. Anonymous, he slipped back inside the council chamber, using a side entrance. Amy followed, keeping to the darkness.

*

'Let me see,' said Hilthe, 'if I understand what you have been telling me. Against my instincts and my beliefs, against all that I know and perceive and understand, you tell me that creatures that are not of my world were the makers of this metal. These strange artists fashioned it into the shape of this beast and later abandoned it here, deep in our soil. All this happened long ago, long before my own people began to live here.' She paused for a moment, closing her eyes very briefly. 'I shall leave aside for the moment the many questions I have concerning the origins of my people.'

The Doctor and Rory exchanged a look of relief. Getting Hilthe to believe in the existence of extraterrestrial life was one thing. Asking her to get to grips with evolution at the same time was probably a bit much for one evening.

'The makers of the beast abandoned it during the course of a war,' Hilthe went on. 'A war which they later lost. My people, discovering the creature, began to work the metal. This has, in some way, called to its makers and drawn them to Geath, like a beacon on a hilltop. Speaking through me, they have asked for the return of their property. But their enemies have also followed the signal and they too demand that the metal is given to them.'

She paused to marshal her thoughts, pressing her fingertips against her forehead.

'Of this faction we know less, other than that they are willing to arouse in the hearts of people great fear and dread. They have been visiting our city for some time now, but this evening, they have at last threatened us directly, and they have shown great powers – they can fly above our heads like huge birds, they can let loose a fire that lights up the night sky and destroys whatever it strikes. Our choices, therefore, seem to be either that we believe the Herald when she claims that her people are trustworthy, or we submit to the threats of her opponents and surrender the metal to these walking nightmares, these Regulators. One way we take a risk, the other we put ourselves in danger. It is an unhappy set of choices.'

The Doctor beamed at her. 'Excellent précis!'

Hilthe raised her eyebrows at him. 'You persist in this misapprehension that I require your approval. But you are in error.'

The Doctor shrugged. 'Just saying. I can see why you did well in this chamber for so long. Till you lost, that is.'

Hilthe frowned at him and turned away.

Rory said, 'But it's not really a choice, is it, Doctor? The Regulator's threatened us, thrown gunships at us. The Herald hasn't. All she's done is ask us to give back what's hers. Shouldn't it be returned to her?'

'Returned to her masters,' said the Doctor.

'Same thing.'

'No it's not,' the Doctor said sharply. 'Masters. Don't like that word.'

'But you saw her!' Rory persisted. 'She was friendly! She was *beautiful!*'

'Appearances? Deceptive? Heard that saying? How about: All that is gold does not glitter? Does that ring a bell?'

Rory appealed to Hilthe. 'You must know! She spoke through you! You must have felt it, too! That it's safe to hand over her Enamour.'

Hilthe did not reply. She was walking slowly round the dragon, brushing her hand along it, contemplating what it might mean.

'An ancient feud,' she said. 'And the city of Geath caught in the midst, between two deadly enemies whose weapons are more powerful than anything yet dreamt of by my people.' Her eyes sparkled. 'You know how this metal works, don't you, Doctor?'

'Yes, I do,' the Doctor said softly.

'Could it...' A tremor of excitement entered Hilthe's voice, and she looked hungrily at the dragon. 'Could it be used to defend us?'

'Don't go there,' said the Doctor, very quickly.

'Could we fashion weapons from it?'

'You could,' said the Doctor. 'But I won't allow

it.'

'No?' Hilthe came to an abrupt halt at the dragon's head. She rested both her hands upon it and began to caress it. 'Is that your choice to make? Do you decide what is best for the people of Geath? Have we fallen so far that we now require a dictator? Why should that be you, Doctor?'

Rory held his breath. Didn't Hilthe have a point? The dragon was here, in Geath. Even the Doctor admitted that it had been on this planet for millennia. So what gave him the right to come in and demand that the Geathians did what he told them? Rory eyed the Doctor. It was all pretty high-handed when you thought about it. Wasn't it just as bad as the Regulator screaming its demands and sending its ships? Or waltzing in the night before a wedding and spiriting away the bride? What gave the Doctor the right to interfere? It was for the people here to decide, and Rory couldn't think of anyone better than Hilthe to make that decision.

'You could try, Hilthe,' the Doctor said very quietly. 'But if you haven't liked the changes in your city so far, I think you'd hate what you saw next. If Geath looks damaged to you now, picture it as a battlefield. Picture it burning. Picture the aftermath – the ruin and grief and the sorrow and the loss. Picture everything you have ever known and loved ripped to pieces and ground down into the dirt. Because that's what would happen. Do you think either side is going to let you take it? You haven't seen half of their power and you can't begin to imagine it. They've got more weapons, bigger weapons, worse weapons. They don't care one jot about your beloved city.'

His voice became very kind. 'I know you hated to lose. I know how much you miss your old life – all the thrill of debate, of talking people down, of winning. And you're right – if you used this technology, you'd get the city back. Everything you lost would be restored. You'd become Queen – but you'd be the Queen of a nightmare. The Queen of Ruin. Is that how you want to be remembered? Is that what you want for Geath?'

Hilthe bowed her head. Her hands were shaking. Rory could see the struggle going on within her.

'That's Enamour, Hilthe,' the Doctor said gently. 'Making you want it. Making you want the vision that it's showing you. But it's lying. And you've lived too long and seen too much to be fooled now by a lie so blatant.'

Maybe it was a trick of the light, but Rory thought there was a faint glow about Hilthe, a trace of the Herald perhaps, as if something of the alien's presence remained within the old woman. All of a sudden, Rory was desperate for Hilthe to take over. More than anything he wanted her to claim the dragon for her own. If Hilthe was the one making the decisions, Rory knew without doubt that he would do anything she asked. 'Take it,' he murmured. 'Take it.'

'Can you hear it, Rory?' the Doctor said quietly. 'Can you hear the dragon? Listen. *Listen…*'

Rory listened – and heard. Faintly, but he heard. The dragon was singing.

'The Queen of Ruin, Hilthe.' The Doctor's voice was hideously discordant against the dragon-song. Rory could have hit him for wrecking something so beautiful. 'Hilthe the Destroyer. They'll sing the name for ever, and they'll curse it.'

Abruptly, Hilthe stepped back. She released her hold on the dragon's head. The music stopped. 'That… was unexpected,' she said. She gave a small and shaky laugh. 'Perhaps you are right, Doctor. It is all so very gaudy. Geath will be better without it.'

Rory gave a sigh of relief. His conviction that Hilthe should take possession of the metal seemed strange now; a delusion, a moment of madness. He shook his head to clear it of any echo and then he frowned. 'Doctor. That humming, that song – it hasn't stopped. It's getting louder.'

'I know,' the Doctor replied through gritted teeth. He ran round the dragon to stand where Hilthe had been only moments before and looked down at the beast's head.

Rory followed him round and stared at the dragon in amazement. Its other eye was opening, revealing a red glow behind a heavy liquid lid. Its jaw began to move. Then, behind the ever-louder song, Rory heard a creaking sound. Looking up, he saw the dragon's metal wings unfolding.

'Doctor, it's waking! The dragon is waking!'

Chapter

7

The Teller took a deliberately complicated route deep into the heart of the council building. It didn't take Amy long to realise that he too was keeping to the shadows and trying not to run into anyone. Perhaps that wasn't surprising given the way the townsfolk had reacted to him in the plaza earlier. Amy wasn't complaining. The Teller had earned their fury, and his sneaking around worked to her benefit.

The corridors became narrower but hardly bare. Enamour covered every wall, pale and uncanny. Eventually, the Teller came to a small arch over which curtains were drawn. He went through.

Amy hurried to the end of the corridor and

twitched one of the curtains to look inside. The room beyond was a private apartment, small but beautifully furnished. A big, comfortable bed dominated the space. Enamour glistened thickly – but only here and there, as if someone started decorating and then lost interest.

The Teller sat down in one of the ornate chairs. He chewed at his thumbnail and muttered under his breath, occasionally glancing over at another curtained arch on the far side of the room. He was clearly waiting for someone. After a few minutes, he jumped up and started pacing from lamp to lamp, taking them out of their holdings and examining them, as if trying to work out some means by which they could wither and die. Some means other than alien intervention.

Amy waited patiently. At last, someone came through the other arch. A man in golden armour, on the breastplate of which was a beautifully stylised symbol of a golden dragon, rampant, on a red field.

The Teller greeted the new arrival. 'Where have you been?' He went to help him take off the helmet. This resembled the dragon's head – or, perhaps, the long muzzle of the Regulator's mask – the nose guard recalling the snout, the cheek plates thrusting upwards in the shape of wings. A red plume rose from the crown. Beol – for of course it was he – looked the very definition of a warrior king.

'Where do you think I've been?' Beol said as soon as he was free of the helmet. 'Ordering the defence of the city.' He placed his hand upon the Teller's shoulder and gave his broad and startlingly beautiful smile. 'And where have you been throughout this crisis, oh wisest of counsellors?'

'Where do you think I've been? Watching your back!'

Beol laughed. 'What would I do without you?'

'You'd have an unguarded back,' the Teller said. 'I've also been gathering information.'

'Yes? Useful information?'

'You're not going to believe the half of it,' the Teller muttered.

Beol walked over to a nearby table, where a jug of water and a cup stood ready and waiting. He poured out some water and drank deeply. 'Don't worry. I know already. The city's mood is changing.'

The Teller blinked. 'What?'

'I saw the crowd out in the plaza. I heard what they were saying. I know that people are frightened.' He shook his head. 'I can hardly blame them. Dragons, fire in the sky, candles and lamps that fade out as if in fear. I understand why they're afraid – I'm not ashamed to admit that I'm afraid myself. These things are beyond reason! But don't worry. I'll do my part. If those beasts come past again, I'll be there. I'll fight. Not just for the city of Geath, but for you.'

The Teller stared at him. 'What are you talking about?'

Beol put down his cup and walked over to the Teller. He rested his strong hands upon the other man's shoulders and smiled down at him. 'You've done everything for me. Our whole lives. But it's my turn now. You got us here. I'm going to keep us here. You don't have to worry.'

From where Amy was standing, she could see the pair of them side on: a tall golden man and a smaller dark one. One of the lamps behind them flickered, altering the composition of the tableau, bringing the profiles of each man into relief. Suddenly, the similarity between them was revealed: the same long nose, the same curve to the chin, the goldish tinge to the Teller's hair, the brownish shade in the King's hair. Amy almost gasped. How had she missed it? These men were so obviously brothers.

'I'm going to protect you,' Beol said. 'I'll always protect you. You have my word, not just as a man, but as King of the Geathians.' He kissed his brother quickly on both cheeks and gave another ravishing smile. Then he moved back into action, the hero of his own story. 'Now,' he said, 'back to my knights. We have an enemy to prepare for and to defeat.'

The Teller stood stock-still in the middle of the room. Beol had apparently taken all the words out of his mouth. After a moment, he shook himself and turned to speak to his brother. 'Beol, you've got to listen to me—'

'Best thing for you is to stay in here till this whole business is over, I think. No point exposing yourself to any danger, whether from the townsfolk or these creatures. Leave that to me.' Beol took another deep drink of water and threw the cup onto the bed. He picked up his helmet again but paused before putting it back on. His face lit up and his eyes shone. This was how Rory had looked, Amy thought, seeing the dragon-ships flying overhead.

'Stars, though!' Beol said. 'Did you see them? If they didn't mean us ill, you'd have to call them beautiful! Swift and supple, like liquid metal across the sky – never did I dream I'd see something like that! Like one of your old stories come to life! You did see them, didn't you? I'd hate for you not to have seen them, even if only the once.'

'Yes, I did – Beol, *please*, listen to me!'

Beol halted on his way back out.

'These creatures,' said the Teller. 'They're not... they're not from our world.'

Beol frowned. 'I don't understand—'

'You've seen them!' spluttered the Teller. 'Where do you think they come from?'

Beol eyed him cautiously. 'It's been a long night,' he said. He nodded at his bed. 'Perhaps you should think about getting some rest. I've told you I'll take care of everything.'

'Beol!'

'Perhaps I should have made you rest sooner. It's been a busy few months. We don't have to turn our attention to Dant immediately. We'll sort out this business first.'

'Dant? You don't seriously think all of this is coming from *Dant*, do you? Beol, those dragons are machines. When, exactly, do you think the people of Dant learned to build machinery like that? How, exactly, do you think they have learned to set fire to the sky?'

'But who else can it be? Who else holds a grudge against us?'

'Beol,' said the Teller carefully, 'you do remember that we didn't *actually* take the dragon from Dant, don't you? That was just a story that I made up. Remember?'

'No coincidence those three turning up tonight, is it? Citizens of Dant? Spies, more like! I'll say one thing before I go, though, you got them wrong. Two children and a fool, you said! Nothing to worry about, you said! Next thing we know – dragons overhead!'

Behind her curtain, Amy winced. Not such a good cover story after all, perhaps.

'Which reminds me,' Beol said. 'Probably best all round if we have the three of them locked up. Can't have three spies from Dant running around the city, if we're likely to be at war by the end of the week.' He tucked his helmet under his arm. 'Enough talking! Back to doing! I can't spend the night hidden away in here. I have to be outside. As soon as the people see their King, they'll be heartened!' He drew back the curtain. 'We knew it was only a matter of time before they came to get it. Don't worry! Nobody from Dant is going to lay a finger on our dragon! It's ours – and ours it will stay.' He nodded towards the bed again. 'Put your feet up. Get some shut-eye. We'll talk again in the morning.' Then he strode out of the room, whistling, a young man confident that his considerable strength would be enough.

The Teller chased after him. 'Beol, we owe these people nothing! You're going to get yourself killed!'

Amy whistled softly to herself. So many stories; stories that had not been true when they were first told, but were now taking on lives of their own, twisting round and turning true... The people of Dant had sent spies to Geath and now they were coming to claim their dragon…

Time to get back to the Doctor and Rory. But could she get there before they were seized by Beol's men? She glanced across the room to the arch through which the two brothers had left. No point going that way; she would only be following them. Most likely she would arrive just in time to see the boys dragged off. She would only end up having to prise them out of the stocks.

'Oh, now that's a tempting image…'

However, and with regret, Amy turned back the way she had come, setting off at a run in search of another, quicker way round to the council chamber.

Her head pounded with unanswered questions: Where had Beol and the Teller found the dragon? Who had they been before arriving in Geath? And who, out of all the parties now laying claim to it, had the best claim to all the Enamour?

As the wings of the dragon extended and lifted, its head bent forwards until the snout almost touched the ground. The wings spread out as the dragon eased them effortlessly apart, gears and metal smooth despite long centuries lying dormant.

The Doctor hung back for a moment. When nothing rose up, writhed forwards or jumped out, he went to see what treasure lay within.

'Ah! Now I understand!'

Reaching inside the dragon, he triumphantly lifted aloft a madly intricate piece of equipment, a tangle of wires hanging down from it like tentacles.

'Emotional amplifier! Now we know why the Teller's been getting such a high level of audience appreciation.'

'Do we?' said Rory, bewildered.

The Doctor, who had been thumping buttons and twiddling dials, peered at him. 'Ah. Of course. No technobabble. Take a guess, Rory. What do you think an emotional amplifier might do?'

Hilthe stepped forwards to peer at the device. The Doctor shook it. It went *ping*. 'Might it amplify emotion, by any chance?' Hilthe said.

'Spot on! Gold star! Second thoughts, not gold. It does indeed amplify emotions. Someone tells you a story and if you're within the range, the whole experience becomes more affecting, more meaningful. I've no problem with them for personal use – they're great for repeats; honestly, you can recapture the experience of watching the first time – but I'm not so happy about them being used on a big audience. And when combined with Enamour…' He gave Hilthe a knowing look. 'No wonder you've had problems getting out the core vote. There's Beol, offering people the kind of riches they've never dreamed of, and there's the Teller, turning the King's exploits into the pre-industrial equivalent of a box-office smash. Good old-fashioned tub-thumping didn't stand a chance. Sorry, Hilthe. If it's any consolation, it's the same old story, wherever you go – the first to get the hang of the new communications medium always wins.'

'No apology necessary, Doctor,' Hilthe said briskly. 'If anything, I do feel slightly better knowing there was no decline in my own abilities.'

'Good for you!'

'But how did the Teller work out how to use this emo-amp-thingie?' Rory said. 'How did he operate it?'

'I don't think he did,' the Doctor said. 'I think the amplifier was on standby, and when he dug up the dragon – whenever and wherever that happened – it reactivated. It would have started working for him without him knowing what was happening. I bet he was amazed to discover his stories were getting such good reception at last. Give him his due – he's known how to make the most of it all.'

'So this must be what the Regulator is using?' Rory said. 'Emotional amplifiers. Only they know how to use them properly.'

'Another not-gold star! Now, the Regulator has been amplifying different emotions. It stirs up fear and anxiety in order to frighten people into doing what it wants. The Teller has been whipping up excitement and enthusiasm. People feel that something special is happening, and they want to be part of it. They want to get close to it.'

'So that's why all anyone can talk about is the King?' Rory said, remembering the Beol-centric conversation in the hall.

'Exactly! It doesn't feel anywhere near as unpleasant as what the Regulator is doing, but it's still a kind of coercion. Most fads and fashions are when you think about it. On top of that, the effects of Enamour aren't stable. People are going to want more and more. They'll want more of the metal and they'll want more impact from the Teller's stories. He and Beol will have to deliver, or else public opinion will turn against them, and the backlash won't be pretty. Emotions are already running high.' The Doctor paused, the amplifier still in his hand. 'Of course, the Regulator will blow us up first. I'd better not forget about that.'

'Please don't,' said Rory.

But the Doctor had returned to rummaging inside the belly of the beast. 'Now, what else do we have here? Ah, this is very interesting…' He popped back out again, carrying a black and silver box topped by an impossibly tiny satellite dish. 'Take a seat, both of you. This is something you should see.'

Rory ran across to the arcade and brought back two chairs, one for him and one for Hilthe. They both sat down. The Doctor played around with the box for a few moments. The dish started spinning wildly. 'That should do it!' He aimed it up at the roof.

Rory and Hilthe both looked up to see images dancing across the dome of the chamber. The colours were richer and deeper than in the images the Regulator had transmitted. Rory burst out laughing. 'IMAX! Nice one, Doctor!'

Hilthe stared at the display in amazement. 'Earlier, the Regulator showed us pictures of my city from above. I do not recognise these places that you are showing me.'

The Doctor smiled. 'I know you don't need my approval, Mother, but I've still got to say... you're very quick. Very quick indeed. No, this is different. The Regulator showed us what was happening outside, right at the moment we were watching. Live broadcast. But these are pictures from the past – from the Herald's past and the Regulator's past. I think if we watch them we'll learn a whole lot more about the nature of the feud between the Feond. Perhaps by the end, we'll have a better idea which one of them should be given the metal.' He glanced at Rory, who was about to answer, and put a finger to his lips. 'Take a look before you say anything more.'

'But, Doctor—'

'Pretty pictures! Free movie!'

Rory sighed, folded his arms, and leaned back in his chair. As he watched, high above him, the story of a brutal civil war unfolded. It was a war that had taken place millennia ago between people alien to everyone in the room. An ancient golden empire, ruled by the Bright Nobles of the Feond, was shredded by a violent revolution. It began on a small world at the fringes of their territory and spread across planets and systems and centuries. The images shifted, and changed, showing the bloodshed on every single one of the empire's thousands of worlds, with the armies of the imperial families on one side, and the militias formed by its servants and bonds-people on the other. They watched as the habitations of the Bright Nobles were torched in the first attacks by the rebels. They saw the bloody reprisals, as the ruling party burned the ecologies of insurrectionist worlds into desolation. They watched the agonies and destruction of total interplanetary war. And they sat through the vicious endgame, when the Imperial Lord of Light himself was at last caught in the catacombs below the Celestial Hall, trapped amongst the bones and the tombs of his ancestors, and was slaughtered with his last loyal legion of Bright Lords. They saw the Thirteen, the representatives of the Oversight Committee, raise their black flag amidst the charred ruins of the Hall and start to squabble over the reconstruction. Last of all, they saw lifeboats disappear into the void of space, the last remnants of the noble households making their escape, fleeing into exile with whatever remained of all they had once possessed, sustained by dreams of a glorious restoration.

The images came to an end. 'A choice between aristocrats and bureaucrats,' the Doctor muttered. 'Why is nothing ever simple?' He glanced over at Hilthe. 'You see now that you made the right decision, Mother?'

'Yes.' She nodded slowly. 'Yes, I do see that now. To use tools such as this, even in defence... Soon enough they would be used in anger.' She shuddered. 'I would not want a repeat of all that I have seen here. Not in Geath. Not for anything.'

'Said you were wise.'

Hilthe tilted her head, permitting the compliment this time. 'The sooner the city is free of these terrible devices the better. Doctor, let me hear your counsel. What would you advise?'

'We have to hand it over to the Herald,' Rory said quickly. 'She hasn't shot at us. Giving in to the Regulator would be like giving in to blackmail.

Wouldn't it? They've threatened us. That's like…
terrorists!'

The Doctor flicked the tiny satellite dish, setting
it spinning like a gyroscope. 'However,' he said,
'the Regulators clearly understand how dangerous
Enamour is. They saw how it was used to control
their people, to maintain that perfect society.
Perhaps that's why they're reacting so strongly.'

Rory appealed to Hilthe. 'Can't you explain?
She spoke through you—'

Hilthe held up her hand to stop him. 'Doctor,
am I correct in my assumption that what we saw
was an account of the war seen through the eyes of
the Herald and her people?'

'Yes, I think that's right.'

Hilthe turned to Rory. 'If we were to ask the
Regulators, we might hear a very different version
of why this war was fought.' She frowned. 'It
strikes me that the Herald chose her vessel and
her mouthpiece very carefully. Who else in Geath
would be so receptive to the idea of a restoration?
Who else in Geath has longed as much as I have
to see the old order return? The Herald and her
masters are plainly very clever. I do not trust them
as much as you trust them. And the reason that I
do not trust is because I am in many ways very
like them.' She gave the Doctor a wry smile and he
smiled back.

'So,' Hilthe said to him, 'returning to my original question. What would you advise, Doctor?'

'First, I think we should get the dragon out into the main plaza. The Regulator said it was monitoring our progress. Moving it would be the best demonstration of progress we could make.' He stared at the dragon for a moment and then started shoving bits of alien wires and technology into his improbably capacious pocket. 'Also, it will be one less temptation round here.'

Rory watched him in disbelief. 'Doctor, how exactly do we go about moving a massive golden dragon without anybody noticing?'

The Doctor threw the amplifier back inside the dragon. It landed with a clatter. He held up a finger. 'Working on that one! Working on that one right now!'

'Doctor, we won't get as far as the front door!'

'Maybe not.' The Doctor pulled out the sonic screwdriver and used it to seal up the dragon again. 'But I'm guessing that the people of Geath might be glad to see the back of the thing. It's hardly been a good night for them, after all.' He bent down to look underneath the dragon. 'Is this thing on wheels?'

'After this evening, I'll admit that anything is possible,' Hilthe said. 'But you'll have to persuade Beol first.'

'Beol,' muttered the Doctor, as he stood up again. 'Don't talk to me about—Ah, Beol! There you are!' He goggled at him. 'What a *spectacular* hat!'

'Doctor!' Beol stood in the doorway of the council chamber, magnificent in his dragon armour and helmet. 'Why am I not surprised to see you here?'

Chapter
8

Beol strode across the chamber towards them. Four of his knights followed him, and behind them came a fraught-looking Teller.

'It is most strange!' said the King. 'Only a few short hours ago my guests were shown to their rooms – the best rooms that I can offer! – and yet here they are, in the dead of night, skulking round the council chamber... What, I wonder, could have brought them here?'

'Yes.' The Doctor jerked his thumb at the dragon. 'Well, that, obviously. And your Teller has already done that joke. Very good, though. Did you think of it yourself?'

Beol glanced at Hilthe. 'I confess that I'm

surprised to find you here, Mother. I thought you held Geath's interests at heart.' Hilthe opened her mouth to protest, but Beol turned away from her to speak to his knights. 'Take them away.'

'Now hold on a moment!' The Doctor ran to take cover behind the dragon, dragging Rory after him. 'Beol, I don't know what you think is going on here, but I can absolutely one hundred per cent guarantee that you're wrong. You're so wrong that right now whole new scales of wrongness are being calibrated simply to encompass the sheer magnitude of wrong… This isn't winning you over, is it?'

'Beol,' said the Teller. 'He's a clown but I think you should listen to him—'

Beol raised his hand. 'I know already what you have to say, Doctor. I admit I do not understand how you have conjured up these strange apparitions, but my Teller has already explained that they are not demons or monsters, but simply mechanical. If men have made them, I can master them.'

'No, no, no!' The Teller clutched his hands to his head. 'That's not what I was saying! That's the *opposite* of what I was saying! Beol, you can't defeat these ships! Not alone!'

'I am the King of Geath, not you!' Beol replied.

Shocked, the Teller took a step back.

'Oh, marvellous, just what my life needs,'

muttered the Doctor. 'Another power-hungry megalomaniac.'

'It falls to me to protect this city,' Beol said regally. 'As we promised.' He put his hand upon the Teller's shoulder. 'You are very dear to me. But I shall not allow you to make me break my word. I have enjoyed all the riches and honours that the people of this city could lavish upon me. Now I shall play the part that they expect from me. I shall do what we promised. What I promised.'

'Doctor,' Rory whispered. 'He doesn't sound power-hungry. He sounds honest.'

'They're the worst kind,' the Doctor said. 'The ones who believe everything they're saying. Next it'll be the special destiny or "I did what I thought was right."'

As he spoke, the dome darkened and the unmistakable shadows of the dragon-ships were visible again through the gold.

'Beol,' said the Doctor firmly. 'This is an enemy that you do not understand. You can't defeat it, not without my help and no matter how much you strut around in a gold hat saying that you can. People will die if you don't let me help – the same people that you claim to be protecting.'

Beol ignored him. 'Take them and lock them up,' he said to his knights. 'Then you two – find the girl. You two – come and join me outside.

We'll show these dragon-folk we're not afraid of anything they can throw at us!'

The knights moved towards the Doctor and Rory, but Hilthe intervened, stepping between them. 'These people are our friends. They are trying to save the city from some terrible enemies. I strongly advise that you pay attention to what they have to say.'

'Yes!' said the Teller. 'She knows! She's seen!'

The King cut her off. 'Mother, I have always held you in great respect. You have been a fine servant of this city and I have honoured you for your long years of dedicated work. But your people and your city would be better served now if you did not allow yourself to be gulled by spies sent to sow the seeds of mistrust amongst us. And it would break my heart to learn that you were part of their plot.'

'Spies?' Hilthe glanced uneasily back over her shoulder at Rory and the Doctor. 'Plot?'

'They are spies sent from Dant,' Beol said.

'Dant?' Hilthe frowned. 'Don't be ridiculous. They're not from Dant!'

Beol addressed the Doctor. 'Who are you, if not a spy from Dant?'

'I'm the Doctor,' he said patiently. 'I'm here to help—'

'If you are here to help,' asked Beol, 'why did you

present my gatekeeper with credentials showing you were an envoy from Dant? Why did you allow me to receive you at court in that capacity?'

'Ah,' said the Doctor. 'There's an excellent reason for that. An absolutely convincing and thoroughly persuasive reason. I just have to think of what it is.'

'Well, Doctor,' said Rory. 'Another fine mess…'

Hilthe said, 'I am sure there must be a reasonable explanation.'

'Perhaps there is,' Beol replied equably. 'Perhaps you can explain, Doctor, where the young woman who was with you before has gone? Did you send her to spy upon us while you made mischief here?'

Suspicion clouded Hilthe's face. Of course, Rory thought guiltily, that was exactly what she had seen – the Doctor sending Amy after the Teller. Hilthe gave him a bewildered look that quickly turned into mistrust and suspicion. Rory's heart plummeted. It hurt to think that Hilthe thought less of him.

The shadows of the dragon-ships passed overhead once more. The dome quaked.

'I have no more time for this,' Beol said. 'I must go out to the city. Seize them. Find the girl.'

'Doctor,' said Rory, 'I think we're sunk.'

'I'm coming to that conclusion myself.'

'What's your plan?'

'Plan?'

'You do have a plan?'

'Of course I have a plan.' The Doctor whipped out the tiny satellite dish, and brandished it aggressively.

'Never in a million years are they going to believe that's a weapon,' Rory said. 'They're pre-industrialisation, not stupid.'

The Doctor put the dish away. 'Fine. Let's go with the other plan. My very first plan and still my very best plan.'

Rory, knowing what was coming next, groaned, 'Oh no…'

'Run!' shouted the Doctor as inevitably as sunrise or entropy.

They ran. They dived across the chamber into the cover of the arcade and sprinted down it, chucking chairs and tables and gold figurines behind them in order to slow down the knights' pursuit. They crashed through some wooden doors and carried on running along a wide curving corridor. Then, all of a sudden, Rory swerved round and started heading back towards the chamber.

'Rory!' yelled the Doctor. 'Not the plan! *Not* the plan!'

'Hilthe!' Rory called to him over his shoulder. 'Beol thinks she's betrayed him! I can't leave her there!'

The Doctor ground to a halt. 'Why?' he said, to the gilded ceiling or fate or simply to the universe in general. 'Why must they be so *wilful*?' He jogged back down the corridor, where Rory was now being held by two of Beol's knights. As the other two advanced upon him, the Doctor pointed towards Rory. 'You can't lock us up! He's getting married in the morning! No? Worth a try...'

Amy watched these events unfold from the shadow of a column at the far end of the room. Rory and the Doctor made their run for it and the knights chased them. Beol left, presumably to get back to the defence of the city, and the Teller dashed after him. Only Hilthe remained, standing with her hands clenched by her side, staring at the dragon. Amy heard Rory, in the distance, shout Hilthe's name. A few moments later, she watched the knights drag both him and the Doctor back into the council chamber. Hilthe took one look at them, turned on her heel and marched off.

As the Doctor and Rory were hauled off, the Doctor protesting loudly and ineffectively, Amy considered what to do next. If she went after Beol's men, she ran the risk of only saving them the trouble of searching for her. Hanging round the chamber was probably not a good idea either since they might well come back this way. Time was running out. They needed allies, quickly, if they were ever to have a hope of ridding Geath of all the Enamour. Amy decided to follow Hilthe. Perhaps if she talked to her woman-to-woman, she might repair some of the damage done. If she could explain the Doctor... but how did you explain the Doctor? He was inexplicable. 'Don't worry about that for now,' Amy muttered to herself. 'Stay on target.'

Outside, the Regulator's ships were making another flypast. Pandemonium reigned in the grand plaza. Once the ships had passed by, Amy heard more angry and anxious shouts for Beol. Then she heard his voice, rising above the crowd, responding to them, and – almost impossibly – calming them, soothing them, inspiring them. By the time Amy reached the far side of the plaza and began to follow Hilthe up some stone steps, she could hear cheering break out behind her.

Hilthe was waiting for her at the top of the steps. 'I don't like being followed.'

'I'm sorry,' said Amy. 'I thought it was the best thing to do.'

'The best thing to do would be to surrender to Beol. That would also be the honourable thing to do.'

'I haven't done anything wrong! And that

wouldn't be best for Geath.'

'How self-serving! Young woman, whatever your paymasters in Dant have promised you, is it worth all this? Our cities have been friends for such a long time! Why should anyone wish to see that change?'

'I don't know,' said Amy. 'I'm not from Dant. Anyway, neither are the ships. Please, believe me. This is serious, much more serious than you realise—'

'Your charlatan friend the Doctor has gone to considerable lengths to convince me of that. Light shows across the dome of the council hall! Tall tales of a civil war amongst the stars!' Hilthe spoke angrily. 'Some sort of mesmerism to make me imagine someone was speaking to me! What a fool I've been! Why did I believe a word of it? Whatever possessed me?'

'But it's all true!' Amy took a step forwards. 'You've seen the ships! Not a light show or a picture – up there, in the sky above you! How can you explain them? I've not been to Dant, but I bet they don't have hardware anything like that!'

Hilthe hesitated and Amy pressed on. 'We only want to help. Before time runs out and those ships attack in earnest. All they've done so far is set fire to a few trees. When they turn those weapons on the city, it will be gone in no time. The whole city, gone! The Doctor can help, but not if he's locked up in a dungeon somewhere. Please, Hilthe! There isn't much time left!'

Hilthe looked up at the sky. The ships were gone, like a bad dream, and only the moon remained, high and full. Hilthe gestured to Amy to follow. 'Come with me. Beol has people out looking for you. We must get you undercover. I'll take you to my house. Then you can explain why, having lied to both me and Beol, I should believe a single word you have to say now.'

That was a tricky one, Amy thought, as Hilthe led her through the streets. It had seemed such a good idea at the time to pass themselves off as locals; a shortcut to the heart of the action. Travelling with the Doctor, always moving on – you could forget that there were consequences to your actions. When Amy had stepped into the TARDIS, she had stepped out of her old life like a snake sloughing off scales. It made everything so easy.

They reached Hilthe's house, dark between the other gaudy buildings. Hilthe led Amy inside and took her to a reception room at the far end of the house. 'Wait here,' Hilthe said. 'I'll have some refreshment brought up. Then we'll talk.'

Hilthe closed the door behind her. Amy paced the room restlessly. 'Stupid place! Dragons and

Enamour and things with claws for hands...' She shivered despite the heat. That was the worst thing about all this, she thought, the sick cold fear that the Regulator induced. All this shaking and quivering – that wasn't how Amy imagined herself. Amy Pond was someone who climbed over walls, and kept a brave Scottish accent going in defiance of the onslaught of Gloucestershire vowels, and took a ride in a time machine because it was there and – well, because you would, wouldn't you? But the Regulator battered through these defences as if they were as insubstantial as mist. It left her feeling frightened and, worse, it left her feeling alone.

'Stupid!' Amy muttered fiercely to herself. 'You're not alone! You're...'

A fugitive in the night on an alien world, with monsters on the loose and footsteps in the corridor. Booted footsteps. In the corridor.

Amy swung round. She heard Hilthe say, 'In here.' She had been betrayed. Worse than that, she had let herself be led into a trap.

'Stupid! Stupid!'

Amy grabbed a chair and shoved it in front of the door, propping it under the handle to delay any entrance. She looked wildly around the room for another way out. She ran to the window, but it was sealed. She shook it hard but it might as well have been barred. 'It's the middle of summer!' Amy yelled at Hilthe. 'Why are your windows locked, you frightful woman!'

The guards were battering at the door. Amy saw a curtain on the far wall and wondered desperately if she could hide behind it. Nothing else to try. She pulled the curtain back to see a narrow staircase. Servants' access. 'Oh, workers of the world unite!' Amy said gratefully and dashed up the stairs as the guards broke through the door.

Amy came out on a bare landing. There was a window at the far end. She ran over and opened it far enough to be able to clamber out onto the roof. She pulled the window down behind her and then set off, half-running, half-scrambling, across the sloping roof. Seeing its edge come up, she judged the distance, made a running jump, and landed cat-like safely on the next house along. She looked back and whistled. 'Wow! Go me!'

Then she saw the guards. They were through the window and in pursuit. Amy ran across the rooftop. 'Great,' she muttered as she crashed past a chimney. 'Now I'm a character in a video game.'

She made it comfortably onto the next building. This had a wide flat roof with chairs and potted plants dotted around, probably very nice during the day. Amy ran to the far side. Her heart sank to see how far the jump was. She ran round the perimeter of the roof in increasing desperation, sweating and panting for breath, but there wasn't any easy way over.

The two guards leapt across easily from the last building. 'Don't be stupid, girlie,' one of them shouted at her. 'You'll never make it!'

That clinched it. Next he'd be calling her a lady.

'Don't "girlie" me!' Amy yelled back. She grabbed one of the potted plants, threw it blindly at her pursuers, and then set off at a run towards the edge of the building. When she reached it, she jumped. 'Geronim–aargh!'

'Why is it always you I'm locked up with?' Rory complained. He was sitting on a pallet, arms folded and legs stretched out, watching the candle burn down. 'It's not fair! It's always you. There was that time on Ariel Station in the zero-g factory. Then again after the thing with the semi-llamas. Oh, and let's not forget the basement in that house in Venice... I mean, it's not that I mind basements or even llama thingies – I don't mind them, not really – it's just that it's the night before my wedding. Couldn't I get locked up with Amy for once?'

The Doctor – kneeling as he had been for the past half-hour in front of the locked door, sonic screwdriver in hand – said, 'Or else with a stripper called Lucy?'

'I didn't know she was coming! Besides, she didn't strip, did she?'

The Doctor gave him a narrow look. 'Only because she didn't get the chance.'

'It still doesn't *count*! Anyway, I'm not the one that kissed somebody else's girlfriend. Fiancée. Good as wife, actually – it's only a matter of hours. If you ever get us back. If you ever manage to open that door—'

'Rory,' said the Doctor in exasperation, 'could you please be quiet for a few minutes? I am trying to carry out an extremely complex technical task.'

'You're trying to open a door!'

'I'm trying to open an extremely complex technical door!'

There was a short silence. Rory sulked at his shoes. The Doctor glowered at the door and wielded the sonic screwdriver like a broadsword.

'It's not as if that thing ever works,' Rory said. 'I don't think it does wood.'

'I'd ask you please to respect the sonic.'

'I don't think it does *locks*.'

'Respect the sonic!'

There was another short silence.

'I don't even know why you're bothering,' Rory said. 'Give it half an hour and Amy will turn up. She always does.'

The Doctor leaned back on his heels and stared

bitterly at the door. Then he sighed, put the sonic screwdriver into his pocket, and stood up. 'Move over,' he said. He slumped down next to Rory on the pallet, crossed his legs at the ankles, and brooded down at his feet.

'The problem is,' he said, after a while, 'we might not have half an hour. Ten standard time units! I ask you! Not only is it a *rubbish* name for a unit of time,' he said this to the ceiling, as if hoping that the Regulator might somehow hear him, 'but it's absolutely no help in letting me know how much time I've actually got!'

'I hate to say it, but none of this would have happened if you'd only handed over the stupid stuff to the Herald when I said we should.'

The Doctor sighed. 'You do realise, don't you, that you're under the influence of a mind-controlling metal? And not only that but you're getting boring. Beyond boring. Boring was our last moment of excitement.'

'My mind is not under control!' Rory shot back. 'And I didn't mean that the way it came out!'

The Doctor pulled a face. They waited. The candle burned lower.

'So what do you think is going to happen?' Rory said in a subdued voice.

'If we don't get out of here? After whatever is left of our ten "standard time units" —' never had scare quotes been so ferociously delivered, 'the Regulator will turn up, guns blazing. Unless Beol has had a miraculous change of heart, he'll ride out to battle, whereupon he will, I fear, be promptly turned into barbecue. Depending upon how much firepower the Herald's people have at their disposal, they will then most likely mount an attack in order to try and seize the metal from the Regulators. The Regulators will fight back tooth and claw. You saw what they were like when they got going. Collateral damage isn't going to be a big concern. If there's anything of Geath left standing in the morning, I'll be amazed.' The Doctor tapped his forefinger against his lip. 'If it's any consolation, you and I are likely to survive the battle because we're probably down deep enough in here. So the only thing we'll have to worry about is being locked in a dungeon with the crumbling tons of a ruined city heaped on top of us. At some point in all this the candle will go out.' The Doctor scratched his nose. 'Does that answer your immediate questions?'

Rory nodded.

'Can I sit and think for a while now?'

Rory nodded again.

After a few minutes, a key turned in the lock. They both sat up, and looked hopefully towards the door. It opened, Amy was pushed inside, and the door was locked again behind her.

The Doctor elbowed Rory. 'Be careful what you wish for.'

Chapter
9

Ten minutes later, the three travellers had brought each other up to speed. They had also considered their options and dismissed each of the plans suggested. Now they sat in a row on the pallet. Amy glowered at a scratch that ran the length of her left forearm. The Doctor turned the sonic screwdriver on and off, on and off. Rory twiddled Hilthe's map between his fingers. The candle burned slowly down. On and off clicked the sonic screwdriver, on and off. Amy glared at the Doctor. He pulled a face, switched the sonic off one more time, tucked it in his pocket, and wiped his sleeve across his forehead. The heat in the tiny room was stifling.

Beyond the locked door, there was a distant

howl. All three looked anxiously as the candle's flame flickered wildly and almost went out. Amy shuddered.

'That'll be the Regulator,' the Doctor said.

The candle steadied itself. Silence fell again, taut and restless.

Rory cleared his throat. 'You know, there's still a chance that Hilthe will come and get us,' he said diffidently. 'I'm sure she will.'

Enraged, Amy leaned past the Doctor to shout at him. 'Will you stop going on about Hilthe! Hilthe is about as likely to get us out of here as the sonic screwdriver! What is *wrong* with you?'

'Mind-controlling metal,' mumbled the Doctor from between them.

'Did you listen to anything I said to you not five minutes ago?' Amy shouted over him. 'Hilthe turned me over to Beol's men!'

Rory raised his hands to placate her. 'I'm sure it was a misunderstanding.'

'I jumped off a roof! I landed in a tree!' Amy brandished her arm at him, scratch and all. 'There's going to be bruises. I'm going to be purple. At my *wedding*!'

'I still think it might simply have been a misunderstanding!'

'Oh, so the two armed guards who chased me over a roof and then dragged me through the streets and down into this dungeon were simply misunderstood? I'm glad we've cleared that one up! I feel much better disposed towards them now I know they were just misunderstood!' Amy glared at the tile rolling around in Rory's fingers. 'Anyway, it's not Hilthe you're really thinking about, it's the Herald.'

A deep crimson blush spread slowly across Rory's face. The Doctor slid out of the way and went elsewhere, not an easy task in so small a room but one to which he applied himself fully. 'That's not true,' Rory lied unconvincingly.

'What is it with you and Golden Girls at the moment anyway?' Amy said. 'First it's the Old Woman of Geath, next it's a gazillion-year-old being of light.'

'You're just jealous!'

'Jealous? How did you work that one out?'

'That you didn't see the Herald first!'

'As if I care two hoots about an addle-brained over-lit—'

'Anyway, what about you, Amy Pond!'

'— Christmas tree decoration! What about me?'

'You and the Ancient Mariner over there! Nine hundred years old, Amy! Nine *hundred*!'

They were nose-to-nose, staring at each other as if they were complete strangers. Amy felt more alone than ever – and it was worse because Rory was there and she shouldn't feel this way if Rory was there. Should she?

'Addle-brained?' Rory said.

'The Ancient *Mariner*?' Amy countered.

Rory blushed again. 'Yes! All right! That was rubbish. Sorry. Best I could manage.'

Amy began to giggle. Rory rested his cheek briefly against hers. He reached down to take her hand and put his other arm around her shoulder. Amy tucked herself into the space and turned to look at him. Rory leaned down to kiss her.

They did that for a while.

'Sorry.'

'Me too.'

'Love you.'

'Love you too.'

'Hate this Enamour stuff.'

'Hate it too.'

They went back to kissing and when they were happy again, Amy rested her head on Rory's shoulder and they leaned back together against the stone wall. 'Doctor,' Amy called. 'You can come out now.'

The Doctor, who had been standing with his back to them and his ear pressed against the door, turned round. Amy and Rory held hands and smiled at him.

'Do you have a plan yet?' Amy asked nicely.

The Doctor put his hands in his pockets. 'I do, in fact, have a plan.'

'Then let's hear the plan.'

'My plan is to wait for whoever is now scratching at the keyhole to let us out.'

Amy and Rory looked over at the door. He was right – there was somebody out there, scrabbling away. Amy squeezed Rory's hand. 'It might be Hilthe.'

Rory kissed the top of her head. 'Doubt it.'

The door opened slowly to reveal the Teller, bent over the keyhole. He looked up at the Doctor. 'Help,' he said.

The Doctor smiled down at him benignly. He pulled the dungeon door wide open and threw his arm out expansively. 'Step into my office.'

'Beol's very brave,' said the Teller, 'but he's going to get himself killed. I don't want him to get killed.'

'Of course not,' said the Doctor. 'Who wants to see their baby brother turned into a crisp by a massive dragon?'

The Teller blinked at him. 'Yes. Quite.'

'So you thought you'd come to me. Very sensible. Best decision you've made all day. Best decision you've made all year.'

'Well, and because of what your friend did

earlier.' The Teller nodded towards Amy. 'In the plaza,' he said to her, 'you put yourself in harm's way for me. You didn't have to do that.'

Amy shrugged. 'I think you've been an idiot, but I didn't think you deserved to be pounded to a pulp.'

'Thank you,' said the Teller fervently.

The Doctor smiled. 'Good work, Pond.'

'All part of the service, Doc. Um, Doctor.'

'So you decided you could trust us, after all?' the Doctor said to the Teller.

'I need you to help me explain to Beol what's going on, in a way that he'll understand. He's convinced this attack is coming from Dant. I think he's planning to declare war on them.'

'I doubt he'll get the chance,' the Doctor said drily.

'Well, exactly! All that I saw earlier, the dragon scale, the flying machines...' The Teller lowered his voice. 'I know this must sound like nonsense, but...' He took a deep steadying breath, and then committed himself. 'I think they've come from another world. I know... I know... I'm crazy, that's what everybody says, always have, but...' He held his hands up helplessly. 'What else can it be!'

The Doctor merely smiled. 'So where did you find the dragon, then? Not in Dant, that's for sure.'

The Teller snorted. 'Of course we didn't find it in Dant. Or Sheal, for that matter. We found it in a field up in the high country west of Jutt. Not too many people up there. Must have been there for ages. Beol saw something glittering and we thought it might be jewellery, something we could sell. So we got digging. Surprised when it turned out to be that dragon, I can tell you. I didn't recognise the metal, so I guessed it was probably rare and, if that was the case, it would be valuable. I was going to break it up, sell it off in bits and pieces. But the first time I did it I realised it was having an odd effect. I had a tiny piece in my pocket one night. Someone called out for a story and I started telling one about a dragon. What else? Nobody ever wants to hear about dragons. But that story – oh, they couldn't get enough of it! I earned more that night than I had done since we left home. Making money from storytelling?' He gave a hollow laugh. 'Oh yes, there had to be something not right about that dragon!'

'And as soon as you realised that, you decided to come to Geath.' The Doctor gave him a canny look. 'Why Geath, of all places?'

'Ah.' The Teller raised an eyebrow. 'Now that is a much longer story.'

'Good story?'

'Of course.'

'Ooh. I like a good story.' The Doctor sat back down on the pallet and crossed his legs. 'Go on, then.'

The Teller gave him an anxious look. 'Are you sure you want to hear?'

The Doctor gestured around the room. 'Captive audience.'

A Much More Likely Story

'I put it to you,' said the Teller, sitting down on the floor in front of them, 'that city-state republicanism is a fine and admirable thing – provided you have the good fortune to be born in one of the cities. However,' he held up a finger, 'should you have the bad luck to be born out in the country, life is not nearly so good. That's where Beol and I come from – up the river, the far end of the Vale of Evesh. Nice country. Excellent fishing. Very fertile all round, in fact. That's important. Because the problem with these great cities,' the Teller wagged his finger for emphasis, 'is that while they're very busy doing politics and making art, they're not producing much in the way of food. Difficult to grow crops in the middle of all this stone. But, given that their citizens get as hungry as anyone else, the cities need to own big pieces of land, and they need to have people working hard on that land while they're off busy—' He pointed towards his audience. 'What are they busy doing?'

'Doing politics and making art!' his audience chorused back at him.

'Well done! Quite. So most of their politics is concerned with these big pieces of land. And most of what goes on between the cities is passing the bits of land around. Like a big game. Only it's not as much fun for the people who are living on that land. They find themselves passed back and forth in treaties like so much loose change. Now, this is precisely what happened in our part of the vale a few years ago. The city of Sheal, our previous owners, blew the latest round of trade negotiations with the city of Geath, and as a result they ended up having to sell off part of their holdings along the Evesh to them at a vastly reduced price. When the land gets sold, the people get sold along with it.' He gave a wry smile. 'It doesn't make much difference most of the time, not really, because on the whole you only ever see city folk when they're there to hand over the deeds to the new owners, and the rest of the time you're still farming the land in exactly the same way... Only this time, it didn't work out that way. This time, the borders changed, and our farm got split down the middle. Well, we weren't too pleased about that, for various reasons to do with tedious technicalities like no longer being able to use the services of the blacksmith over the bridge and having to go miles upriver instead…'

'Bureaucrats,' muttered the Doctor darkly.

'Quite. So we decided to make our opinion known.' The Teller frowned. 'Now over the years I've found that my little brother Beol comes in handy in those sorts of situations. I stand him next to me while I'm talking, and people are usually too busy worrying about him to do anything but agree with what I'm saying. This time, however, the citizens of Geath had rightly predicted that there might be some trouble. So they sent a few big strong boys along with their administrator.

'Now,' the Teller looked at the Doctor. 'Nobody wants to see their baby brother turned to a crisp by a giant dragon.' He glanced at Amy. 'Neither do they much like seeing him pounded to a pulp by goons. When he *could* stand up again, I decided that we weren't going to be passed around ever again and that we were going to find a better way of life. So off we went. After half a year wandering around and not eating very much, the dragon turned up. When it turned out to be so useful, I decided it was time to pay a visit to Geath.' He frowned down at the ground. 'Sheal was next on my list.'

Amy bit her lip and glanced over at the Doctor. He was leaning back against the wall and his face was in shadow. Quietly, he said, 'It's all true, you know.'

The Teller looked up. 'What's true?'

'Other worlds. Other beings. Travel between the stars. Universal suffrage. All true.' The Doctor leaned forwards. He was smiling. 'Just thought I'd mention it.'

The Teller closed his eyes. A slow smile – of pleasure and delight – crossed his face. Amy could see clearly the dreamer he must once have been, and probably still was at heart.

After a moment, the Teller opened his eyes, rubbed them, and cleared his throat. 'Well. Of course, that means for certain that Beol can't defeat these star-dragons by strapping on his armour and waving his sword at them. Not that he listens to me any more.'

'He's started to believe his own publicity,' Amy said. 'The townsfolk aren't helping. You've done too good a job.'

'If you have any suggestions,' the Teller said drily, 'I'm ready to hear.'

'Suggestions?' said the Doctor. 'I'm full of suggestions. Bubbling over with them.' He jumped to his feet. 'Now that the locked door is no longer an issue, for which my grateful thanks, I think we have three main problems. Firstly, we are caught in the middle of an ancient interplanetary civil war between deadly enemies equipped with equally deadly weapons. Secondly, we have an as yet undetermined amount of time to collect up every single piece of Enamour currently lying around the city of Geath. *Thirdly*,' he took a breath, 'if Beol by some miracle does manage to fend off both the Herald and the Regulator, he will start a war with Dant and the three of us could well be executed as spies.'

'Don't worry about that one, Doctor,' the Teller said. He was clearly starting to enjoy himself. 'I'll put in a good word for you.'

'For that, amongst other reasons, I am indeed not going to worry about our third problem – well, not until tomorrow morning at least. But! There's a long way yet till morning! And in the meantime, bearing in mind our most pressing problems, I suggest we do the following. Firstly, we make a start on gathering up the metal.' He pointed at Rory and the Teller. 'That'll be your job.'

'What will we be up to, Doctor?' Amy said.

The Doctor folded his arms. 'I'm going to get that dragon if it's the last thing I do.'

Rory covered his face. 'You mustn't say things like that! Not out *loud*!'

'Doctor,' said the Teller slowly, the magnitude of his task beginning to dawn on him, 'the whole city is covered in Enamour. How can we possibly collect it all? We can't knock on every single door in Geath. The Regulator won't have given us that much time, surely?'

'I have an idea about that,' said the Doctor. 'Well, it was Hilthe's idea, really. She set me thinking. She was on the right lines when she said that we could use the Feond technology in some way. Where she got it wrong was in wanting to make weapons. We'll never win that way – not least because I suspect both sides would incinerate us at the first sign of trouble. Besides, that's not what Enamour is good at. And it's not all that we found when the dragon opened up.' He started rummaging around in his pocket. 'You're right – you can't knock on every door in Geath. However long we've got, I doubt it's long enough to do that. But there's something else that we can try. Where is that thing…? Ah, here it is!'

He pulled out the impossibly tiny satellite dish. 'While you were chasing around town, Amy, Rory and I took in a movie.'

'Oh, very nice.'

'You wouldn't have liked it. Things exploding. People dying. Depressing.' He looked down at the dish, which he was cradling lovingly in his cupped hands. A green light was flashing on the side. 'I used this as a projector. But it isn't just a projector, it can also work as a transmitter.' The Doctor pressed a button. The green light went off and a red one came on. 'If I set this up correctly, the metal should act as a receiver, for whatever we transmit. There's Enamour in every single home around the city by now. What you need to do,' the Doctor nodded at the Teller, 'is to tell people to bring whatever they have out to the main plaza. Amy and I will go and get the dragon and when the Regulator comes to collect, all of the Enamour will be out in the open, ready and waiting for them… If I decide that they've earned it.'

The Doctor looked round, expecting applause and finding only bafflement. 'It's perfectly simple! You've no imagination! All right, let's show not tell… Amy, pass me that hideous brooch you seem to be wearing all of a sudden.'

'What?' Amy looked down at her shirt. 'Oh! Yes!' She unpinned the brooch (it truly was hideous, what had she been thinking?) and handed it over.

The Doctor placed the brooch on the far side of the pallet. 'Keep watching that.'

He pointed the satellite dish at Amy and played with the controls. A tiny, crackly image of Amy appeared above the brooch.

Amy began to laugh. 'Help me, Obi-Wan!' she cried. 'Oh, I've always wanted an excuse to say that.'

'How can we be sure people will hand the stuff

over?' Rory said. 'Doesn't it make them want to keep it?'

The Doctor turned earnestly to the Teller. 'This is where you come in. I need you to talk. Talk like you've never done before. You're going to tell the best story you've ever told, the story of your life. Tell people they have to give up the metal. Tell them why. Get them to bring it out.' Seeing the Teller's doubtful expression, he said, more urgently, 'I know you can do it. You're a natural. You turned your little brother from a serf into a king!'

The Teller shook his head. 'Doctor, we both know it was the dragon that did that.'

'No, *you* did it. All your idea. All your words. I heard you in the council hall! You were magnificent. And it's exactly like I told you – all that Enamour did was to amplify your voice so that people couldn't help listening.' He held the dish out. 'This will make your voice stronger than ever before. And what you'll be telling is a better story than any you've told before. Because it's going to save the lives of every single person in this city.'

The Teller stared at the satellite dish. 'Let me see if I understand what you mean. You want me to speak to the people of Geath and explain that they must surrender the metal at once. That they should bring it to the grand plaza in front of the council chamber. You want me to impress upon them the urgency of this and the terrible danger they will face if they do not comply. And, somehow, this tiny metal bowl will be able to take my words and the images I conjure up with them, and place them into every single house in the city of Geath.'

The Doctor gave him an appreciative look. 'You and Hilthe! You pick this stuff up so fast! I'm impressed! Yes, that's exactly what I mean.' He placed the dish with ceremonial care into the Teller's hand. 'Take care of it.'

Amy, who had been staring at her own image, turned to the Doctor. 'Television. You're going to save the world through television.'

The Doctor grinned at her. 'How else?'

'Doctor, you're brilliant! It'll never work.'

The Doctor put a hand over a heart. 'I swear it will be a ratings triumph.'

As if it could not bear to hear any more, the candle went out. Only the red button on the satellite dish remained alight, flashing away like a warning sign.

'Telly-*what*?' said the Teller; a lost, bewildered voice in the darkness.

Chapter
10

Outside their cell, the corridor was empty. One torch burned dimly.

'I sent the guards out to help with the defence of the city,' the Teller said.

'Good thinking,' said the Doctor. 'An instinctive revolutionary. Why you got mixed up in king-making I'll never know.'

The Teller led the three travellers quickly and quietly back up into the main levels. They came to a point where the corridor branched and the Teller pointed to the right-hand passage. 'That way leads back to the council hall if you're serious about stealing the dragon.'

'Not stealing,' said the Doctor primly. 'Saving

Geath from itself.'

'Semantics,' coughed Rory under his breath.

The Doctor pointed in the other direction. 'Don't you have a live broadcast to make?'

Rory turned to Amy. 'No unnecessary risks, OK?'

'You know me!'

'Yes. That's what I mean. That's exactly what I mean.'

'Don't worry, I can take care of myself!' Amy said.

'Hmm.' Rory kissed her on the cheek. The Teller was plucking at his sleeve and giving him an assortment of impatient glances. Rory squeezed Amy's hand and followed the Teller down the left-hand passage. When he looked back, Amy and the Doctor were already lost to the shadows.

Rory and the Teller went along dark passages empty even of Enamour, heading steadily upwards. They came out, in time, on the far side of the main plaza.

Rory glanced back down at the council building. 'How long exactly have you been in Geath? Didn't take you long to map out all the secret passages, did it?'

'They're access tunnels for messengers,' the Teller explained. 'A quick way in and out of the hall. Very useful. And,' he admitted, 'at the back of my mind, there was always the fear that we would find ourselves driven out of town.' He led Rory up a stone staircase. 'How about here? Will this do?'

Rory looked back down into the plaza. Yes, it was a good spot. They would see very quickly whether or not they were having any success. 'Great! Perfect!'

'So what do we do now?'

Rory placed the satellite dish carefully down on the flagstones.

The Teller tapped it doubtfully with his toe. 'It's so small. Are you sure this is going to work?'

Rory, who was deeply unconvinced, said, 'Oh, the Doctor's a genius! His plans always work.'

'Hmm,' said the Teller.

Rory pointed the dish at him and operated the controls in the sequence the Doctor had shown him. He looked at the wall near the Teller, where a panel of beaten Enamour would, he hoped, act as a monitor. A fuzzy image of the Teller's face appeared on the flat surface. Rory laughed. 'Blimey! It does work!'

The Teller stared at himself and touched his cheek. 'Do I really look like that?' he said in horror.

'Camera adds a few pounds.'

'And everyone in Geath can see me?'

'I hope so. Don't worry! You look fine!' Rory

turned a dial and focused in on the Teller's face. 'Come on! On with the telling!'

The Teller gaped like a fish. 'What do I say?'

'Try "bring out your Enamour". Only, you know, say it properly. Go on! Go for it!'

'*Everyone* in Geath?'

'Absolutely everyone,' Rory said cheerfully.

The Teller blanched. 'People of Geath,' he whispered.

'Bit louder. I know – pretend it's only me. Talk to me.'

'People of Geath,' the Teller said, more loudly this time, although somewhat hoarsely. Rory put his thumb up in encouragement and the Teller took heart. 'People of Geath. Like me, you have seen remarkable events unfold this evening. Like me, you must have wondered where these great flying creatures come from and why they wish us harm. And in your hearts, like me, you must know the answer already.' The Teller clasped his hands together and leaned forwards, becoming more confident as the urgency of his message surpassed his nerves. 'You know how this trouble has arisen. The riches that we have all enjoyed belong to others. Now they have come to claim it back. So we must return it. We are not thieves! We must give back to these visitors what is rightfully theirs. Whatever you have – bring it to the grand plaza.'

The Teller held up his left hand. One by one, he took off the array of rings. 'We all must make this sacrifice,' he said. 'I shall be first. Please! Follow my lead! Bring all that you have to the grand plaza.' He held out his palm, showing the rings lying there. 'Bring it quickly!'

Rory nodded enthusiastically. He glanced down towards the plaza. There wasn't much movement there yet, but he supposed they hadn't been going for long and perhaps it was taking people some time to get used to the idea of a pocket-sized Teller talking to them in their own homes. 'Keep going!' Rory mouthed. 'You're doing great!'

The Teller had barely started to repeat his message before they heard the drone of engines across the valley. He pointed at the sky. 'The star-dragons! They're returning!'

Rory looked up. Two distant specks of light shone above Geath. As he watched, they began their approach. They hurtled like lightning along the valley and across the city at such close range that Rory ducked instinctively as they passed directly overhead. 'Wow!' Dragons or dragon-ships – both were awesome, both were terrifying. 'Come on!' he yelled to the Teller over the roar. 'We've got to keep going!'

The Teller made his broadcast again and, to Rory's relief, he saw the first signs that they were being heard and understood. A dozen or so people ran into the plaza, dumped armfuls of Enamour near the steps of the council chamber, and then ran off again – Rory hoped – to collect more.

'We should show them you mean it,' Rory called to the Teller, pointing down at the collection of rings.

They ran down into the plaza and the Teller threw his rings onto the pile of goods accumulating there. 'See!' he cried. 'All of us! We all have to do this!'

As he spoke, an inhuman howl rose up, like metal scraping across the soul. A dark figure took shape at the far side of the plaza. The Teller turned frantically to the transmitter. 'Please!' he begged the people of Geath. 'You've got to listen! You've got to do what I ask! We don't have much time! Bring out the metal!'

Rory turned the dish towards the Regulator. Perhaps if people saw it, even indirectly, they would grasp that it wasn't made up, the Geathian equivalent of an urban myth. The Regulator shot up until it towered over the council building, blotting out the gold haze rising from the dome. Rory trembled under the influence of the emotional amplifiers. The dish shook in his hands. The image of the Regulator wavered in and out, but its demands boomed out across the valley and directly into every home in Geath.

'I represent the Regulatory Board. Under Clause 9.4b (subsection 12.2) of the Regulation of Psycho-Manipulatory Metals Act (30673.26) all parties here assembled must hand over any substances covered by said Act. Under powers granted to the Regulatory Board by the Regulation of Psycho-Manipulatory Metals Act (30673.26), reasonable force can be used to secure all substances covered by said Act.'

'Do what it says!' The Teller's shout was barely audible over the Regulator's wail. 'Bring it out! Bring it out!'

But the plaza was empty. Everyone had fled before the Regulator and nobody dared to come and confront it. Except one man.

Beol rode out. His armour flamed gloriously in the darkness, unaffected by the Regulator's power. He galloped across the plaza until he was face to face with his enemy. He reined his horse back, stood up in his stirrups, and lifted his sword.

'Be gone, foul monster!' he cried. 'Leave my city in peace!'

'Oh, Beol,' his brother whispered. 'Don't get yourself killed now.'

The Regulator bore down on the King. 'Surrender the Enamour!' it bellowed.

'Never!' cried the King. He brandished his

sword, spurred on his horse, and galloped headlong at the Regulator. Rory, still trembling in fear and excitement, held up the satellite dish and captured the moment, showing it to the whole of Geath. The King rode straight through the Regulator. It flickered wildly and then disappeared. Beol, turning for a second pass, saw his victory and threw his sword up into the air. He caught it with ease.

The people of Geath flooded into the plaza. A chant rose up: *Beol! Beol! Beol!* Even Rory, knowing it was a projection, almost cheered along with them. Then he saw the Teller's face.

'What did you do that for? They'll never listen to me now!'

Rory frowned and scratched his head. 'What are we going to *do*?'

Amy and the Doctor stopped outside the side entrance leading onto the arcade. The Doctor opened the door a crack and they both peered inside. The dragon slumbered in the centre of the hall. 'Right,' whispered the Doctor. 'What do you want to do?'

'Why are you asking me?'

'You're the one that kept talking about heists.'

'*Doctor!*'

However, Amy didn't get to speak her mind.

The Doctor grabbed her arm and pointed at the dragon. On its Enamoured flank, a face was coming into focus. Rory's face, somewhat larger than life.

'I know he's my boyfriend and all,' whispered Amy, 'but that's *scary*.'

'Doctor!' Rory's voice boomed out around the hall. 'Are you there? We've got a problem!'

The Doctor put his hand to his forehead. '*Secretly* steal the dragon, is what I said. Which part of "secretly" is so difficult to understand?'

'Is it working?' asked the Teller.

Rory stared unhappily down at the satellite dish. 'I have absolutely no idea.'

'I know I'm not an expert,' the Teller said, hesitantly, 'but how can he reply? Does he have one of the bowls too?'

Rory sighed, bent down, and picked up the dish. 'No.'

'So what now? We've got to keep them bringing out the metal.'

Rory pocketed the dish. 'What we need is someone that's at least as good as you at getting people to do what they want. Seems obvious to me. We need Hilthe.' He caught the Teller's expression. 'Oh, don't you start!'

'I feel I should I point out,' the Teller said silkily, 'that I *easily* defeated Hilthe in the last election.'

'True, but then she's not the one that's caused two massive dragon-ships to come screaming over the city and raining fire down on it. I think her stock might be up.'

The Teller stopped complaining, but he hardly looked happy.

'Come on,' Rory said. 'Hilthe-wards.'

'What shall we do?' Amy whispered. The huge image of Rory's face flickered and then disappeared.

'We'll sneak over to the dragon,' the Doctor whispered back. 'Open it up. See if there's another dish. He has to go and talk to Hilthe. Get her to help.'

'Oh, he'll like hearing you say that! All right, lead on.'

They came out of the cover of the arcade and tiptoed towards the dragon.

'Halt! You're under arrest!'

Four of Beol's knights stepped out of the shadows, short swords drawn, and advanced on them. The Doctor ran, weaving around the columns of the arcade. Amy dived in the other direction, drawing away two of their pursuers.

'I have to talk to Beol!' shouted the Doctor as he helter-skeltered round a pillar. 'He has to listen! Why won't any of you listen? Is it the jacket? The mud's your fault! You should pave your roads! Is it the bow tie? Is it the *face*? How many times do I have to say it? Appearances can be deceptive! I'm nine hundred years old, you know!'

Rushing past the main doors to the hall, the Doctor crashed straight into Beol, on his way in. 'There you are! About time!' He smoothed down his jacket and straightened his bow tie. 'What does a man have to do to get an audience around here?'

Beol seized the Doctor's arms, spun him round, and pinned him up against the wall of the chamber.

'You have to *listen*!' said the Doctor, voice somewhat muffled now that his face was pressed up against gilded stone.

Amy, at bay behind the dragon with two knights advancing on her, yelled at Beol, 'Stop being such a cloth-headed stupid lump of muscle and let the man *speak* to you!'

Beol looked at her with a rather hurt expression and then, suddenly, his face changed.

'What?' Amy said. 'What is it? Why are you looking at me like that?'

'Amy!' cried the Doctor, trying to release himself from Beol's grasp.

Amy looked down at her hands. Gold light was transforming the flesh on them, turning them translucent.

The Herald was coming – only this time she had not waited to be summoned.

In sheer fury, the Doctor wrested himself free of Beol's hold. He ran across the council hall, but could not get close enough to the Herald to try to pull Amy back. Besides, it was already too late. Amy was enveloped in golden light. A strident harmony was building up, echoing off all the metal in the hall.

Beol ran over to the Doctor. 'What's happening?' he shouted.

The Doctor ignored him. 'Let her go!' he yelled at the Herald. 'This is a crime, a terrible crime! You don't have her permission! Get out of her body!'

The Herald turned to face him, white light flashing from Amy's eyes. 'We have waited long enough,' she said, her voice harsh and belligerent, a terrible distortion of Amy's. 'Surrender the Enamour or we will destroy you. We will destroy this world.'

Beol grabbed the Doctor's arm. 'What's happening? What has happened to your friend? What is this apparition?'

The Doctor swung round to face him. 'This is your enemy!' he shouted at the young man and pointed at the Herald. 'Not Dant, not Sheal! *This*!

The enemy of us all! A power that uses other people as a means to her own ends! A mind that can only think of others as tools, as possessions!'

'I know that enemy,' Beol said simply. 'What must I do to defeat it?'

The Doctor did not reply. Digging into his pocket, he pulled out another device taken from the dragon earlier. It was a small black box. He dived forwards to set it on the floor a few metres away from the Herald and aimed it towards her.

'What are you doing?' said Beol. 'What is that?'

'This will defeat her,' the Doctor said, quietly, fiercely. 'It's done it at least once already.'

A low howl rose up from the box.

Beol started. 'I have heard this sound before many times.'

'Watch,' said the Doctor.

In bare seconds, a dark shape appeared and began to rise up, hands outstretched for the Herald.

Beol, horrified, turned to the Doctor. 'But this is the beast I defeated only moments ago!'

The howling got steadily louder, the scream of an angry, wounded animal. The King pressed his hands against his ears.

'Defeated it?' The Doctor laughed hollowly. 'It was an illusion, Beol! They can make as many of these as they want. They'll keep sending them down here to scream at you until you beg them to take their dragon back. But they'll set the city on fire first!' He had to shout to be heard over the cacophony, the discord between the Herald's martial music and the shriek of the Regulator that he was creating. 'Your victory was an illusion, Beol! You were never in danger!' The Doctor bent down over the controls, directing his Regulator to begin its assault on the Herald.

The Herald reacted violently. She raised Amy's hands and sent waves of the golden rings of light out across the hall. They struck the two knights closest to her and sent them flying. They crashed against the big stone columns and fell to the ground, bodies crumpling as if they were nothing more than dolls thrown away by a spoiled child in a fit of pitiless pique. Beol ran to them, but the Herald, catching his movement, turned her wrath towards him. She lifted Amy's hand and prepared to send out another bolt of deadly light. Only the Doctor, turning the Regulator upon her, prevented Beol from being killed. The King took cover behind one of the columns. The Doctor turned back to the Herald and pressed his assault.

Trapped within the Herald's sphere of influence, Amy knew from the moment that the Doctor put the box on the ground that his projection would only make matters worse for her. Close now to the Herald's mind, closer than she ever wanted to be, she knew that the presence of the Doctor's Regulator served chiefly to enrage her. The Herald, Amy knew, would never let her go as long as the Doctor threatened her, and perhaps not even then.

Tears rolled down Amy's cheeks as the alien used her hands to deliver the lethal blow that blasted Beol's knights across the hall. 'Switch it off!' she whispered, but her voice was overwhelmed by the Herald's cruel song.

The Herald turned towards Beol, lifting Amy's hand against him, but the Doctor's Regulator pushed her back. The Herald recoiled and cried out in thwarted agony. Amy seized her chance. Summoning every ounce of her will, she screamed at the Doctor, 'Switch it off! Switch it off! It hurts!'

The Doctor heard. He gave Amy an anguished look, then grabbed the black box and thumped it. His Regulator subsided and disappeared.

But the Herald was not going to let Amy's act of defiance go unpunished. She turned all of her will and her fury inwards, battering against Amy's defences, her sense of self. Now Amy felt the impact of the emotional amplifiers in the hands of an expert, manipulated by someone who knew exactly how to wield this technology. This was their full power, not the haphazard and accidental effects achieved by the Teller, and aimed at stimulating a terror vaster and more consuming than anything even the Regulator had tried to produce.

All the uncertainty and apprehension that Amy had experienced since arriving in Geath, all the fear and loneliness she had tried to battle, surged through her, magnified a thousand-fold. All her sadnesses were amplified and turned into the theme of the Herald's song. The delights were drowned out; the sweet moments of joy that not only make life bearable but make it everything that it is. The Herald sang over them until only the sorrow remained.

Amy's knees buckled; her soul buckled. This, she understood now, was how the Bright Nobles created their empire and kept their age-long rule intact. They had done it through fear, through separation, trapping their subjects in the isolation of a gilded changeless hell. Amy felt herself sliding into that chasm, horrified and enthralled in equal measure, unable to stop herself and uncertain that she even wanted to.

Faintly, through the Herald's empty and encroaching music, Amy heard the Doctor. 'Fight it, Amy! Fight it!' But his cry grew more distant and his voice became that of a stranger, someone she had never really known. She was 7 years old again, waiting for the man who had said he would come back and take her away, the little girl lost, sitting in the garden waiting for a knight in shining armour who had not returned. Amy pictured herself standing on the edge of oblivion and there was nobody to help her.

Only herself. 'I'm not afraid of you,' Amy told the seductive void opening within her. 'I'm not yours. I'm me. I'm Amy. And I'm not alone!' She clenched her hands; hers, under her control. 'So you'd better stop using my body before I *really* lose my temper!'

Chapter
11

There was a blinding flash. The rings of light engulfing Amy pulsed outwards. She convulsed under the recoil and the Herald's grip on her slackened. It felt to Amy as if iron bands that had been slowly tightening around her chest – choking her breath, choking her self – suddenly slackened. Keeping this picture in her mind, Amy imagined herself gripping hold of the bands, pulling them apart, throwing them away. The chasm that, only moments before seemed to be opening ineluctably before her, started to recede, like a bad dream shaken off by the coming of morning.

But the Herald would not give up easily. She made a last grab for control of Amy – to seize her, if she could not persuade her – amplifying the harmonies until the hall itself throbbed with the noise. Amy sang back, random snippets of songs, anything that came to mind. With one last effort, and a rousing rendition of 'Twinkle, Twinkle, Little Star', Amy released herself. She pushed the Herald back for good – away, and out of her mind. The gold light shot upwards, coalescing in a ball high above. The Herald screamed in fury and outrage; sheer white noise that cracked the dome. Then she was gone.

'Ta-da!' Amy said, and fell to her knees.

She put her hands out to stop herself falling on her face. The Doctor and the King ran to help her. Amy stretched out her arms and let them lift her back to her feet.

Beol bent over to kiss her hand. 'You are a lady of great courage.'

'I'm not any kind of a lady. But if you do that smile again, I'll forgive you.'

Beol obliged.

Amy wrinkled her nose at him. 'So cute! I'd vote for you.'

The King placed his hand upon his chest and bowed to her. Then he went to see to his knights.

The Doctor pulled her into a hug. 'I'm impressed, Pond. You're impressive.'

'I know.' She smiled at him. He smiled back. He

had come back, she thought – just later than he'd said. Still a mistake, though, to sit around waiting for the knight in shining armour. There was the whole of her life to be led.

'What did you see?' the Doctor said softly. 'Can you talk about it? What did she show you?'

'A bad place. The worst. A place where nothing changed.' Amy shuddered. 'For thousands and thousands of years, nothing changed. There was Enamour everywhere. It was in the food you ate, the water you drank, the air you breathed. It shaped everything around you, totally. It slid into every space. You were like a bird trapped in an oil slick. Trapped in a beautiful golden oil slick.' Then there had been the humming, the lulling… but behind that, almost extinguished but still constant, the whispering of fear… 'More than anything you wanted to get away from it, but you didn't dare. Where could you go? There was nowhere to go. You couldn't make a move, you couldn't get out, you couldn't save yourself… And – this was the worst thing – part of you wanted to stay there. It wanted what was on offer. Craved it. Not changing. Not having to grow. Handing that over. It felt like security – but it wasn't, not really. It was hell. A golden hell.' Amy sighed. 'I didn't defeat her, did I? Not entirely. She's coming back.'

'I'm afraid you're right.'

'Then I suppose we'd better be ready for her.'

The Doctor nodded slowly. His put his hands in his pockets and walked to the centre of the hall. He looked up at the dome, where the Herald's light had glowed moments before and where now only a long crack zigzagged from one end of the dome to the other.

Amy joined him. 'You feel sorry for her, don't you?'

'Hmm?'

'The Herald. You feel sorry for her.'

'Hmm.'

'Why, Doctor? Why bother?'

'I suppose...' Still staring at the crack, the Doctor screwed up his face. 'Because she's as trapped as anyone else. She has her masters, after all, and she's answerable to them. If she fails here in Geath, what will happen to her?'

'She has a choice, too, Doctor. She could refuse to obey her masters.'

'That's much easier said than done.'

'The Regulator's people did it. The Herald doesn't have to obey these Bright Nobles, does she? Not now. Not so long after the end of their war.'

'The Bright Nobles.' The Doctor's face screwed up in distaste at the name. 'Now, they're the real villains of the piece, aren't they? I wonder how bright they really are, without Enamour. The Herald may be a few rungs up the ladder from the great mass of servants, but she's by no means at the top.'

Amy thought about this. She thought about the Herald's pitilessness, the casual cruelty with which she had been seized and used. She thought about the strident music and the dead sound of despair at the heart of it. Was that also part of the Herald's song? 'You know,' Amy said slowly, 'I think those extra few rungs make all the difference.'

Beol came back to join them.

'How are your two knights?' the Doctor asked.

'Dead,' Beol said grimly. 'Both dead. Their bodies broken.'

'Still sorry, Doctor?' Amy murmured.

'Always sorry, Amy,' the Doctor replied. To Beol, he said wearily, 'Are you going to listen now?'

'You have no need to speak. The metal must go.' Beol glanced towards the heart of the chamber, at the source of it all. 'The dragon, too. But not to the Herald's people.'

'No, not there,' the Doctor agreed. 'To the Regulator, then.'

'You're not with happy with that, are you, Doctor?' Amy said.

The Doctor shook his head. 'Rory might have been speaking under the influence of Enamour, but he was right when he pointed out that the Regulator has threatened us. Handing it over feels too much like being coerced.' His eyes flashed. 'And I don't like being coerced.'

'But it's the only option, isn't it?' Amy said. 'Unless you're planning to take it yourself.'

The Doctor glanced back over his shoulder at the dragon.

'The howling creature has made its position clear,' Beol said firmly. 'The dragon must be delivered to it, or else Geath will suffer. We cannot allow that.'

'Doctor,' Amy said, 'you might know as well as the Regulator how to dispose of the stuff, but I don't think that's the point.'

For a fraction of a second, the Doctor seemed to be somewhere else, lost in contemplation. Then: 'Nah. You're right. Imagine it in the TARDIS. Doesn't suit the new colour scheme, does it?' Shaking off whatever vision had briefly entranced him, he bounded off towards the doors. 'Come on! Time to check on Operation Dis-Enamour.'

Rory looked up at Hilthe's back window with a familiar sinking feeling. He clasped his hands together and braced forwards. 'Step on here,' he said to the Teller. 'I'll push you up then you can reach down and pull me up.'

'Do you break and enter often?' the Teller asked in a censorious voice.

'Do you overthrow legitimate governments and install puppet rulers often?'

'Not under normal circumstances.'

'Well then. There's your answer. Alien invasion. All bets are off. Besides, the window is open, so technically it's not breaking and entering. Now hurry up. I don't know how long we've got left but I'm guessing it's not long. It'll be morning soon.'

The Teller made no further protest and stepped onto Rory's hands. Rory pushed him through the window, and then reached up so that he could haul him inside.

'Where will she be?' whispered the Teller, looking down a dark bare corridor.

Rory pointed ahead. 'Amy said there were some stairs. They should be up there, on the right. They lead down into a sitting room and chances are Hilthe's not getting any sleep tonight. Plus we've got an escape route back here. You know, in case.'

The Teller nodded in agreement and Rory led the way down the corridor. They found the narrow flight of stairs by which Amy had escaped earlier that night. The doorway at the bottom of these was covered in a curtain. Rory twitched it aside and looked into a sitting room. It was the same one he had visited. Was it only a few hours since he had sat here, drinking sweet tea with Hilthe, and got his first sight of the Herald? He was sorry he had ever set eyes on her.

Rory pulled back the curtain and quietly entered the room with a degree of stealth that would have won plaudits from the Doctor. Hilthe was sitting in one of the chairs, eyes closed, apparently asleep. Rory turned to the Teller, put his finger against his lips, and then gestured to him to come in. The Teller tiptoed across the room and stood in front of the door.

'Now that my escape is blocked,' said Hilthe, her eyes still closed, 'who will strike the killing blow? Will it be you, Rory?'

'What?' Rory said, shocked. 'What do you think I am?'

'A spy. An assassin.' Hilthe opened her eyes and glanced over her shoulder at the Teller. 'I see now that this plot has been a long time in the making. But before you dispatch me, I would like to know the price. How much were you paid by the people of Dant?'

The Teller rolled his eyes.

'For heaven's sake!' Rory said. 'How many times do we have to say this? *We're not from Dant!*'

Hilthe's eyes flashed. 'What other explanation can there be?'

'Mother,' said the Teller, 'I beg you, for a moment,

try to look beyond the petty concerns of the city-states of the Evesh. I know they've kept you busy for a lifetime, but they are trivial compared to the crisis we face tonight.'

Hilthe glared back at him in loathing. The Teller did not move from his position in front of the door. He folded his arms and glared back.

'Um, we were supposed to be winning her over?' Rory said. 'Remember that bit? Getting her on side?'

'I have no interest in winning this woman's favour,' the Teller replied bluntly. 'She has done nothing to make me want it.' He turned back to Hilthe. 'You were right in your estimation of me, Mother. I do hold this city in contempt. I came to Geath to take revenge. And I've enjoyed every moment. I've loved watching the people hang on my every word. I've loved watching them want to get close to me and to my brother. I've loved their devotion and the knowledge that whenever I chose, I could ruin them.'

'Will you shut up?' hissed Rory. 'We need her help!'

'No, I won't shut up!' the Teller said. 'I won't be quiet any longer! She's going to hear this! The Doctor told me to talk like I've never talked before, to tell the story of my life. Well, the story of my life is that the council of this city – of which you were the leader, Hilthe! – broke up my home and sent men to beat my friends and family into submission!'

'So you *are* here to kill me,' said Hilthe. She raised her chin defiantly. 'I'm not afraid. I would *die* for Geath.'

'Kill you?' The Teller came to stand very close to her. 'It's what you expect from me, isn't it? You think I'm good for nothing, don't you? A thug from up the river. Not a soft-handed citizen like yourself. And so I am. I'm country-bred and I'm proud of it. But *kill* you? I've more on my mind tonight than you! I'm trying to save your city! I'm trying to set right a bad mistake. Where have you been tonight, Mother Councillor? Sitting in here, clinging to the past—'

Hilthe sat bolt upright in her chair, proud and angry. 'How *dare* you! A farmhand from the valleys! What do you know of Geath's glorious past?'

'I know enough!' the Teller shot back. 'I know it's not as glorious as you make out! And I dare because it's true! You say you'd do anything for Geath, but that's all talk! If you truly loved your city and its people and its long history, you'd put aside your pride and you'd come with us now, not hide away in the moment of its greatest need. Die for Geath? My *brother* is willing to die for Geath. My brother the King.'

The Teller stopped speaking. He backed away from Hilthe and went to lean back against the door. He was trembling with emotion. Hilthe sat with her hands folded before her and her head bowed. Rory could not see how angry she was, but perhaps there was something he could still say to persuade her.

'Hilthe,' he began hesitantly. 'We really do need your help. We're not spies, we're not enemies, and we're trying to do the right thing. But we need your help.'

'Please, Mother,' the Teller said. His tone was much gentler. 'Let us set aside our differences. The people of Geath have put themselves in our hands. We have to do right by them. I know that you believe I took your power unfairly—'

Hilthe winced.

'You're right,' the Teller went on. 'I did. And I'm sorry. But we are in desperate straits and the people in our care need you. They need to hear your voice again. Please, come and speak to them.'

Hilthe lifted her hand to stop him speaking. To Rory, she said, 'Ten standard time units.'

Rory nodded.

'And we still don't know what one standard time unit is?'

Rory shook his head.

'And you're not going to kill me?'

Rory opened his mouth to protest, and then caught the twinkle in Hilthe's eye. 'No,' he said. 'That definitely wasn't on the agenda.'

'Then I suppose we ought to hurry.' Hilthe rose from her chair. She took a long look around the room and then she strode towards the door. When she reached the Teller, she stopped and looked him up and down. A slow and not wholly grudging smile crept across her lips. 'You do have a great gift,' she said. 'I hope, when this is over, you'll put it to better use.'

'Second chances all round,' said the Teller. 'We should each of us be grateful.' He opened the door and stepped back so that Hilthe could sweep through majestically ahead of him.

'Hurry up!' she called back to Rory and the Teller from the corridor. 'No time to lose! Follow me!'

On the way back to the plaza, Rory explained the satellite dish to Hilthe and what he needed her to do. She clearly didn't believe a word he was saying, even when he demonstrated how the transmitter worked and projected her image onto the enamel of the steps, but she didn't raise any objections. 'If you claim that this will work, I shall take you at your word.' She contemplated her own face. 'Strange metals, strange noises – and now strange devices. A very strange tale.' She twitched her collar straight and smoothed down her cap of silver hair. 'Shall we begin?'

Facing the dish, Hilthe gave a smile of great beauty. 'My dear friends,' she said. 'It is a pleasure to be able to speak to you again, even in a time of such suffering and confusion. You know what it is that I must say to you. You know what has caused us such grief. The metal, my dear friends. The metal. And I am speaking to you now to ask you to give it up. Dear friends, I know how hard this will be, but it has to be done. Only then will Geath be restored to itself. Only then will we be safe.'

As she spoke, Rory kept a close eye out for activity below. As he watched, first one person, then another, darted out, carrying an armful of jewellery, or a pile of golden plates, dumping them in front of the chamber and hurrying home to collect more. Rory gestured with his thumb so that Hilthe could see what was happening.

'Already I see that many of you are answering my call!' Hilthe cried. 'My dear friends, I knew that I was right to put my trust in you! Hurry, please! Bring the metal to the grand plaza! Remember that the true wealth of our city has never been in riches or display, but in kindness, generosity and a desire to live a full and varied life. A life that everyone in the city or under her protection deserves.' She looked at the Teller as she said this, and rested her hand briefly upon her chest, in a silent promise. The Teller nodded to show that he had understood. 'So let us give up this strange metal,' Hilthe went on. 'Geath does not need it! Let us restore our city to its true self!'

Watching the steady trickle of people entering the plaza, Rory felt for the first time optimistic about their chances of success.

The Teller gave him a hopeful smile. 'I think it's working,' he whispered.

'She's a natural politician,' Rory said. 'Knows how to get people to hand over their money.' He played with some of the controls on the satellite dish, and found some of the images of the war that the Doctor had shown him.

'See what happens when this metal is allowed to cover everything around it,' Hilthe said. 'Dear friends, I do not mean to frighten you, but I cannot hide the truth from you.'

Watching the grand plaza so closely, Rory saw Amy and the Doctor the second they emerged from the council chamber. Leaving the satellite dish and Hilthe under the Teller's direction, he ran down the steps and over to Amy. Before he reached her, Rory knew what had happened. There was the same aura, the same faint pearlescent after-image that had surrounded Hilthe after the Herald spoke through her. They reached each other and hugged. 'Are you all right?' Rory said. 'What happened?'

'Amy beat the bad guy!' the Doctor carolled.

'I thought there weren't any bad guys?'

'Did I say that, Rory? I did? Well, this time there is! And when I say "Amy beat the bad guy", what I mean is "she fended it off for the moment". The Herald will be back. How's your Enamour-collecting going?'

Rory turned to Amy. 'What really happened?'

'The Herald decided to make me her mouthpiece.' Amy pulled a face. 'I decided I wasn't having any of it.'

He hugged her even harder. Why had they quarrelled earlier? Why did they ever quarrel? She was brilliant. He would never quarrel with her again. Probably.

'Here's Beol,' said the Doctor quietly.

Rory and Amy turned to look. The King walked slowly down the steps into the grand plaza. Behind him, his knights carried their two murdered comrades on biers. Behind them came the dragon. The crowd of people stopped piling up their possessions and bowed their heads in respect. The dragon shone beneath the moon; heart-stoppingly beautiful and infinitely desirable. Rory felt a pang of regret that it was leaving. Perhaps it always felt this way when an enchantment ended.

'I hope the Teller is getting all this,' the Doctor said, watching Beol's progress.

'I think he must be.' Rory pointed at the pile in front of them, which was working as a receiver. Beol's image appeared above it, and Rory was able to watch both transmission and real event, as the King came towards them.

When Beol reached the pile of treasure, he stopped. He raised his hand and the cortège halted behind him. The carriers lowered the biers and the dragon to the ground.

'Enough,' Beol said simply. 'It is not worth the price. It is not worth it.'

He stripped off his dragon armour and added it to the pile. He placed the helmet on top and took a step back. He looked no less extraordinary without it. Then he bowed his head to his fallen knights.

'Ratings winner,' Amy said sombrely.

The King had barely finished his small ritual, when the people of Geath began to converge upon the plaza, carrying their Enamoured possessions with them. A little girl staggered under the weight of four huge candlesticks. Beside her, her grandmother brought a golden bedpan, which she placed like a cap on the top of the dragon helmet. Soon Beol's armour disappeared from sight, completely covered with the riches that the city was relinquishing. A team was despatched to strip the veneer from the dome of the council chamber. Throughout the rest of the night, as the full and distant moon passed across the sky, the people of Geath stripped their city bare.

At last, a massive heap of golden metal, as big as an earthwork, dominated the main plaza. The whole city had come to see what would happen next, no longer able to watch the images the Teller had steadfastly transmitted or hear Hilthe's firm and friendly encouragement. They filled the remaining space in the plaza, backing onto the stone stairways that led up the hill. Others hung out of the windows of those grand houses that overlooked the council buildings.

The moon set. A brief chill descended upon the city; a still silent moment before the dawn. Then came the distant whine of engines and the unmistakable makings of the Regulator's howl. The crowd shivered, en masse. The two gunships soared across the valley, beautiful and lethal. In the very centre of the plaza, right beside the dragon, the Regulator started to take shape.

From his vantage point on the steps leading up to the council chamber, the Doctor watched its appearance with a cold eye. 'I do hate being coerced,' he said. Then he went forward to hear the Regulator's claim.

Chapter
12

The Regulator grew until it towered over the council building.

'All parties assembled here. Your ten standard time units have now elapsed. In accordance with Clause 9.4b (subsection 12.2) of the Regulation of Psycho-Manipulatory Metals Act (30673.26), you must now surrender all substances covered by said Act.'

Its great voice boomed round the bowl of the valley and, when some people screamed, the Regulator responded with a nightmarish screech that froze the heart and drowned out all competition. One of the knights' horses – terrified beyond understanding at the monstrous apparition ahead and scared beyond anything that its rider could do to soothe it – bolted into the crowd.

It was nearly a disaster. It was still a tragedy. The crowd scattered as best it could in the confined space but there was a danger that people would get crushed.

'Stay calm!' cried Beol. 'Clear away as quickly as you can! But stay calm!'

People pressed back against each other in order to open up room for the panicking horse to ride through. The rider, bravely keeping her nerve, guided her horse as best she could through this space, trying to keep it from trampling anyone. The poor frightened beast, seeing no way clearing ahead, did not respond to its rider's soothing words and gentle hands, and came skidding to a halt, its hooves slipping on the stone. The rider was catapulted from its back and crash-landed against a pillar with a sickening crack.

A terrible hush followed. Rory sprinted over to the knight but it was clear to him at once that she was dead. Behind him, the horse, trembling and snorting, was caught and steadied. Rory closed the young woman's eyes. A gabble of talk broke out, turning quickly from confusion into anger, as the townsfolk grasped that they had complied with all the demands made of them but one of their number still lay dead.

The Doctor rounded on the Regulator like a force of nature. He ran across the plaza and came to a halt in front of the giant creature. 'Is this your new order?' he shouted up at the monster. He flung out his arms, encompassing the plaza and the whole city of Geath. 'Is this what you wanted? Striking terror into the hearts of people who can barely understand your powers? Driving them to death through fear? Is this why you fought your war?' Quietly, turning away with a wave of the hand, he delivered his final blow. 'You're no better than the masters you rejected.'

The Regulator hovered silently above. Amy held her breath. The crowd, too, grew silent again; people were watchful and fearful. Had the Doctor gone too far? Was this the moment when the reprisals started, that reasonable force that the Regulator had promised? The whole city was here. It would not take much for the two gunships to wipe out every living thing in Geath.

As Amy watched, the Regulator shrank. When it was roughly human size, it took a step or two to stand before the Doctor, almost as if it was coming forwards for judgement. Its form, too, altered subtly: the sharp edges smoothed; the long muzzle, the fierce hinged jaw, and the extended clawing hands all changed. Soon quite an ordinary humanoid stood there; a little more elongated than

Amy was used to and with a few more fingers than seemed to her to be strictly necessary. The Regulator's carapace was obviously armour; sleek dark armour, worn as much for protection as for show. The alien reached up and removed the helmet. Amy leaned forward for a closer look. The alien shook out long dark braids and lifted her head. Her cheeks were reddish-brown and wet. The alien was crying.

'We meant you no harm!' the alien said. The moonlight glistened on her tears. 'This was only meant as a display of strength.' Her voice, without the modulation that had hitherto been making it come out monotone, was distraught. She looked around the plaza to where the horse was still stamping and snorting. 'Is the soldier dead?'

'Yes,' the Doctor replied flatly.

The alien wiped her gloved hand across her face. 'We meant you no harm.'

The Doctor pointed at the dead knight. 'Yet harm is what you've caused.'

The alien shifted her helmet from hand to hand. 'Don't you understand? We have to remove the metal, as quickly as we can!' she said urgently. 'There might be others in league with the Herald that would seize it before we have the chance to take it. That's why we use these tactics! Enamour binds itself to people's souls! We could not risk a delay. We could not risk being refused—'

'All you had to do was *ask*.' The Doctor pointed at the council chamber. 'That building, there – that's where their council meets. That's where their King holds his court. You could have sent a delegation. An envoy. An embassy! Whatever name it is your committee cooked up for its representatives. You could have talked to these people. You could have explained. Instead you sent gunships!'

'They harmed nobody! We only fired over the city!'

'No more excuses,' the Doctor said coldly. 'They only make me angrier.'

The alien lowered her head in shame. After a moment, she burst out, 'If you had lived all your life with Enamour you would understand!'

'How does that justify what you've done here?' the Doctor shot back. 'You've terrorised these people! Isn't that what your masters did to you? Isn't that how the Bright Nobles ruled you?'

The alien jerked her hand up in front of her face, as if making a superstitious gesture or warding off a blow. 'Don't say their names to me,' she said. 'Don't lecture me about that! You can know nothing about it! The old world, the old order – I lived there! I lived under it!' Her voice became stronger and more passionate. 'If you had lived under their rule, you would understand! Ten thousand years in their thrall – a world without change, without hope, even hope of extinction… Only *Enamour*…' On that word, her voice struck a note of deep despair. It was clear to everyone listening where the Regulator's howl originated and what it articulated. The death of hope. 'We meant no harm. But we will not let anyone keep and use Enamour! There will be no more Bright Nobles. Never again!'

'I understand,' Amy said. She put her hand upon the Doctor's arm. 'Doctor, I saw that world. I felt what it was like. They must have looked down on Geath and seen Enamour spreading out everywhere. They must have been afraid that nobody would pay any attention. If you could cry out like that for ten thousand years and have nobody listen, why would you think anyone was going to listen now?'

'Amy,' the Doctor said gently, 'when they looked down on Geath from their huge and staggeringly well-equipped ships, weren't they able to see at the same time that there was nothing on this world to equal their technology? Couldn't they see that there was nothing here that could be used as a defence against their firepower? Perhaps they thought all of these people didn't matter enough to treat fairly? Did they see a primitive people and think they could come and take whatever they wanted? I *hate* that. Hate it.'

'We don't have to agree with what they've done,' Amy came back. 'We just have to understand.' She paused. 'And there's the Herald. She'll be back soon. We have to decide what to do with all the metal before the Herald comes back.' Amy's voice became urgent. 'Doctor, I don't think there's anyone standing on this world right now that knows better what Enamour can do than the Regulator and her people. Look at her.' The Regulator looked back, eyes bright with tears. 'I don't think there's anyone standing on this world right now that I'd trust more to take care of it.' She gave the Doctor's arm a squeeze. 'You got I was including you in that, didn't you? Yeah? In case I wasn't clear?'

'Thank you, yes, I did grasp the wider point,' the Doctor said. To the Regulator, he said, 'I think you should take your hoard and your war elsewhere.' The alien bowed her head in acknowledgement. As she turned away, the Doctor raised a finger. 'But.'

'Doctor…' Amy said warningly.

'*But*,' the Doctor said emphatically. The alien swung round to listen. 'Earlier, you issued a series of directives to the people of Geath,' said the Doctor. 'And the people of Geath complied with them all. Now they should come under your jurisdiction. Under your protection. Because the Herald will be back and I don't doubt for a second that when she finds out that we have handed the metal over to you, there'll be reprisals. I can't allow that. I can only hope that you won't allow it either.'

The alien shook her head. 'I'm not authorised to make decisions about the deployment of military force—'

'*What*?' the Doctor cried. 'That's not an answer! Is it against protocol or something? Oh, yes, much better to let an entire world of innocent bystanders become *charcoal* than break some ludicrous little rule—'

'*I'm* not authorised to do it,' the alien said and pointed up at the ships, 'but my superior *is*. You need to talk to her. I can transport you to the ship and you can make your case to her.' She nodded at Amy. 'It might be advisable if you were one of the party.'

'Come on board one of those ships? Yeah!' Amy nudged the Doctor. 'Someone from Geath should be there too.'

'Yes, good point.' The Doctor looked wildly around the assembled crowd. The people of Geath stared back uncomprehendingly. 'Who should come? Who here keeps a cool head when faced with almost inexplicable events and has a proven track record of success at high-level diplomatic negotiations?'

'That'll be Hilthe,' Rory said at once.

The Doctor waved his hand in dismissal. 'You always say that.'

'I think this time he's right,' Amy said.

The Doctor stared at her, then at Rory. 'I think this time you're right. Where's Hilthe?' He swung round and called out. 'Hilthe! Your moment's come!'

'So jealous,' muttered Rory.

'What?' Amy said.

'You get to see inside one of those dragons.'

'They're not dragons.'

'Dragon-ships. Whatever. Still jealous. Officially jealous.'

'I'll bring you back a souvenir.'

'Thanks. Um, nothing gold.'

The crowd parted to let Hilthe through. The alien conferred briefly with her colleagues via her communicator and then beckoned to Hilthe, Amy, and the Doctor to step forwards.

'Don't worry,' Amy said to Hilthe, just before the field from the matter transmitter enveloped them. 'Everything will be fine.'

'Of course it will,' the old woman said briskly, as if this was an everyday occurrence. 'It's simply a question of finding a form of words acceptable to everyone.'

*

The matter-transmission field stabilised and Amy got her first sight of the interior of the dragon-ship. They had arrived at one end of a long room filled with ranks of desks. Low partitions made of a pearlescent material placed here and there separated small groups of workstations. Occasional pot plants strove to flourish under the unremitting glare of the fluorescent lights. One of these was on the fritz. An elongated humanoid in elongated humanoid overalls stood on a small stepladder beneath it, fiddling with what Amy hoped was not a sonic wrench. 'Doctor, it's a cube farm.'

'Yes.'

'Like an office.'

'Yes.'

'In space.'

'Everything's better in space. Office space... Ooh, watch it, here comes the welcome committee.'

Three aliens approached. They wore smart-casual and distinctly non-military suits in nearly uniform shades of bluish-green.

The alien in the centre of the group stepped forwards to speak to them. 'My name is Anwa,' she said. 'I'm the chief sub-director of Department Four of the Regulatory Board. I'm the senior representative here of the Reconstruction Oversight Committee.'

Department Four? Amy glanced round. Was

that the name of the ship? It hardly captured the dramatic splendour of the dragon-ship's exterior. The Doctor was right. They were rubbish at names.

Anwa studied each of them in turn. Her eyes were the colour of amethysts. 'Which of you is senior management?'

Hilthe rose to the occasion. She swept past the Doctor and Amy, and delivered an elegant and nuanced bow. With great formality, she said, 'My name is Hilthe. I speak for the citizens and the sovereign of Geath. I greet you with amity and I pray that we part in concord.'

Anwa gravely bowed her head. The two women sized each other up for a moment, and then each gave the other 'I-think-we-can-do-business' smiles. Anwa looked at the Doctor. 'And you are…?'

'Ooh. Good question! I suppose I'm an independent observer. Yes! Like that. An independent observer.' Grandly, he said, 'I shall observe and if pressed I might even provide advice. Independent advice. Independence guaranteed.'

'And you?' Anwa said to Amy.

'I suppose I'm… the independent observer's lovely assistant.'

Anwa pondered the pair of them for a moment and then gestured with a many-fingered hand for them all to follow her. 'Let's get you signed in.'

She led their party over to a desk where temporary passes were issued and signatures and arrival times collected. As this lengthy business and its attendant paraphernalia were sorted out, Anwa took the opportunity to speak to the alien who had brought them up to the ship. They held a brief hurried conference. Amy eavesdropped without compunction.

'There's going to be an inquiry, of course,' Anwa murmured. The other alien's shoulders slumped; her whole demeanour depressed. 'But we're behind you all the way, Camba. The whole department's behind you.'

'I've been saying for *years* that something like this was going to happen,' Camba hissed. 'But all I ever get back is – ooh, well, Protocol Nine Six One was established for a *reason*, can't go messing about with it. Well, I've had it with Nine Six One. I'm not going to operate under these constraints again! This is supposed to be a professional organisation! Professional? It's a shambles!'

'We'll sort it out,' Anwa whispered. 'Start filing your report. They'll do away with Nine Six One this time round, I promise.' She turned back to her guests. 'All done? Let's proceed.'

'I wish we'd brought the Teller,' Amy whispered to the Doctor as they followed Anwa through the office. Elongated people peered over the partitions, trying to get a good look at the alien visitors. 'He would have loved this!'

'He doesn't need to see it.' The Doctor tapped his forehead. 'It's up here already.'

'Hey, Doctor, did you hear them talking about that Protocol Nine One Wotsit?'

'Nine Six One. Yes. Shush. Working on it.'

Anwa led them into a meeting room dominated by a huge round table. They all shuffled round and took their seats. In the centre of the table there was a pile of a pens and a plate of sandwiches. Amy nudged the Doctor. 'Are they sandwiches? Can you get sandwiches in space?'

'Why wouldn't you get sandwiches in space? They're very convenient.'

'Doctor! Space sandwiches! I'm having one of those!'

Amy reached to take one. The alien sitting beside her yelled, 'Don't eat that!'

Amy yanked her hand back. 'Why what's wrong with it?'

'They're stale.' He was faintly embarrassed. 'If I'd known sooner we were getting visitors, I'd have got some more sent up.' He paused for a moment, thoughtfully. 'Maybe some cake.'

Anwa took her seat and called the meeting to order. 'If I can begin by offering, on behalf of all members of the Department, our deepest regrets as to how events unfolded this evening,' she said, apparently sincerely. 'The Department prides itself on the professional service that it offers and I personally assure you that we shall be undergoing a thorough investigation in order to determine exactly the errors that were made and how such errors can be avoided in the future up to and including a thorough re-examination and potentially even revision of all relevant procedures.'

Hilthe – who had been looking increasingly baffled through this short speech – said, 'You mean you're sorry our soldier is dead, and you're going to do your best that nothing like that happens again?'

Anwa blinked. 'Yes. That's what I mean.'

Hilthe raised an eyebrow.

'The Department's sorry,' Anwa said. 'I'm sorry,' she added quietly.

Hilthe nodded slowly. 'On behalf of the citizens of Geath,' she said gravely, 'I accept that apology. I believe our, er, independent adviser,' she nodded at the Doctor, 'has already pointed out that much suffering and distress could have been avoided if you had simply approached us in a more, ah, *conventional* manner. Could my protest be noted for the record?' Hilthe glanced around. 'We are keeping a record of this meeting, aren't we?'

The Doctor whipped out a spiral red and black notebook and proceeded to scribble away in what Amy assumed would be flawless shorthand. The alien on the other team carrying out the same task leaned over and whispered, 'Doesn't your assistant do that?'

'Shocking handwriting,' he said back, traducing Amy without shame. 'Don't know what these schools do with them for all that time.'

The alien tutted and shook her head. 'League tables,' she said darkly and went back to her minutes.

'Your protest is noted,' Anwa said to Hilthe.

'Then let us begin,' Hilthe said.

The whole meeting took slightly under an hour; what that was in standard time units, Amy couldn't say. Her attention drifted once or twice, chiefly to the prints that were hanging on the walls, which depicted jaw-droppingly dramatic alien landscapes. Ebony waves crashed upon silver shores. Vast bridges connected huge towers, built from metals Amy could not name and with engineering she could not guess at. Presumably these pictures looked bland through the eyes of the people here and served chiefly to soothe the nerves during a long afternoon.

By the end of the meeting, Hilthe had negotiated temporary status for Geath as an associate member of the Reconstruction Oversight Committee, with all the rights, privileges, and protections arising from that status. In lay terms, that made Geath and the Reconstruction allies, and the gunships would remain in local space for the duration of the crisis.

'I have another request to make,' Anwa said. 'I will understand if you refuse. It would help if one of your people could summon the Herald again, rather than one of the regulatory team. We've learned from experience that Heralds are able to detect if one of our species is summoning them.'

'That seems acceptable to me,' said Hilthe. 'Doctor, you do still have that ring?'

The Doctor put down his pen. 'I do – but you should think twice before putting it on again, Mother.' He glanced at Anwa. 'This encounter will be for real this time, won't it?'

Anwa nodded.

'For real?' said Hilthe. 'Was it not real before? Explain, please, Doctor – for one who may lack the detailed knowledge to understand how such tricks occur, but who does not lack wits.'

'Each time the Herald has appeared before,' the Doctor explained, 'she's been a projection. She used you – and Amy – as a means of communication.'

'We were her mouthpieces,' Hilthe said, nodding.

'That's right. But this time she'll take full shape.

And whoever is holding that ring will become the channel through which the Herald will pass on her way to taking that shape.'

'I'll do it, Doctor,' Amy said.

'No you will not do it,' Hilthe and the Doctor said simultaneously.

'No, my dear,' Hilthe continued. 'It is Geath that has made this alliance. Geath requires this protection, and therefore Geath will provide this service. And since I am the one that the Herald chose as most likely to share her mind and be persuaded by her appeal, I shall be the one through whom she will pass.' She reached for Amy's hand. 'But I would hear your counsel, for you have defeated her once already.' She drew Amy aside.

The Doctor turned to Anwa. 'Protocol Nine Six One,' he said. 'Rules dictating appropriate forms of interaction with species designated as falling below standards set for extraterrestrial contact. Rubbish protocol. Don't care what you do – reform it, redraft it, dump it – but next time you find a spot of Enamour on a pre-industrial world, *talk* to them! If they're not ready to accept you as aliens, they'll assume you're fairies or enchanters or something. Might try and burn you, but your armour should get you out of that. Anyway, drop Protocol Nine Six One. If you need to talk to them, they should know who you really are.' He wrinkled his nose.

'Non-interference? Prime Directives? So twenty-third century. All a bit retro. And not in a good way.'

'You know it's a poor protocol, Doctor,' Anwa replied, 'and I know it's a poor protocol, and Camba certainly knows it – but try telling my boss.'

The Doctor ripped some pages from his spiral notepad. They were full of closely written notes. 'My independent advice. Been to a lot of places, made a lot of first contacts. Try that on your boss.' Softly, he said, 'Your case stands or falls on its own merits, Anwa. No need to go around terrifying people.'

Anwa took the sheets of paper with a grateful smile.

'I do have one request to make in return,' the Doctor said. 'But first of all – tell me what plans you have for the Herald once you've taken her.'

'We have a procedure for that, Doctor—'

'Yes, I'm sure you do, but you have to admit that not all your procedures have been terribly well thought-through.'

'Fair comment.' Anwa gave a dry smile. 'We'll take her home. She'll be imprisoned, but only for as long as her dependence on Enamour lasts. We have people who will work with her to help her, a whole Rehabilitation Board—'

'So you won't execute her.'

Anwa recoiled. 'We're not murderers, Doctor!'

'But you will use force to capture her?'

'We'll have to. As soon as she knows we're here, she'll come out fighting.'

'Then I must have the chance to speak to her.' The Doctor's voice was low and earnest. 'To reason with her. Make her understand. Because there's a city full of people down there that she can turn on. I don't want them hurt. But most of all, I want to talk to her because I think she doesn't know.'

Amy, overhearing, gave him a puzzled look. 'Doesn't know what?'

'That the Bright Nobles are dead,' the Doctor said. 'That none of them survived.'

Startled, Amy said, 'But she said they were coming!'

'Either she lied,' Anwa said, 'or she's fantasising. Her masters are dead. The Doctor's right. They all died at the end of the war.'

'All of them?' said Amy. 'Are you sure?'

'Oh yes,' Anwa said softly. 'We're sure.'

'Then I must have the chance to speak to her,' the Doctor said again, and urgently. 'Before you try to take her by force. Perhaps if I talk to her, she won't come out fighting.' Seeing that Anwa was shaking her head, the Doctor carried on quickly, 'She's afraid of you, Anwa. She's been alone for a very a long time, without friends, without comfort of any kind. You know that you mean her no harm, and I know it – but she doesn't. She's terrified, but worse than that, she's *powerful*. She could do a lot of damage before you're able to stop her. I bet that's happened again and again in the past.'

Anwa gave a grudging nod.

'See? Those procedures! Sometimes it's worth trying something new. So if I can talk to her, make her come with you willingly, we might prevent more damage, more death. And it might be better for the Herald too. Because if she does stand down, then the battle to free her from Enamour will be half-won. You'll be saved a lot of hard work.'

Anwa sighed. 'After so long, I doubt the Herald knows where Enamour stops and her own self starts. But there's no reason why you shouldn't try, Doctor.'

The Doctor beamed at her. 'That's all I want to do. Try.'

'Still,' said Anwa, 'Camba will be guarding your back.'

'I've no objection to that.' The Doctor looked around the room. 'All done? Meeting adjourned?'

'Meeting adjourned,' said Anwa.

Amy pointed at the pile of pens on the table. 'Anyone mind if I take one of those?'

Chapter
13

Camba transported them back to the main plaza in Geath. When the crowd saw Hilthe, a great cheer went up. She waved grandly in response. Beol came to greet her and bent to kiss her hand. When he gave her his matchless smile, she smiled back, patted his hand, and tucked it under her arm.

Rory nudged Amy. 'Start of a beautiful friendship.'

'Her and her toy boys,' Amy said. 'Never mind, you've still got me.'

'Is the city safe now?' asked Beol.

'We have one last task to perform,' Hilthe told him and held out her hand. 'The ring, please, Doctor.'

The Doctor rummaged in his pocket. 'Still think that I should do this.'

Hilthe waggled her fingers at him. *Hand it over.*

The Doctor sighed and pulled out the ring. It lay small and innocuous in his palm.

Beol frowned down at it. 'What is the meaning of this?'

Hilthe, retrieving the ring, told him, 'We have secured our alliance. Now we must honour its terms and work with our allies to defeat our common enemy. Stand back, all of you.'

They all moved back. Camba put her helmet on and faded into the darkness behind the dragon. For the third time, Hilthe cupped the ring in her hands.

'Come!' she called up to the sky. 'Come back! I wish to speak to you!'

A soft whisper sweetened the night air.

'Come back!' Hilthe called. 'I am here! I am waiting for you!'

The whisper took shape and became a single note. Light formed in Hilthe's hands.

Beol, understanding suddenly what was happening, strode forwards. 'No! I forbid it!'

He reached to take the ring from Hilthe's hands but waves of golden light burst outwards in all directions, preventing his advance and enveloping Hilthe entirely.

'Dear foolish boy,' Hilthe said. 'I am not yours to command.' Holding up her hands, she summoned the Herald. 'I am here! I am waiting to receive you! I have gathered your possessions! Now bring me my reward! Restore my city to me!'

The single note grew in volume. It stretched into a full chord, sweet and melodic, but Amy could hear the terrible hollow echo at its heart. 'Oh, be careful!' she cried to Hilthe. 'Please, be careful! Don't let her trick you! We're all here! I'm here! Remember! Don't forget!'

As Amy watched, the old woman's body went rigid and her flesh became translucent. She saw at once the difference between her own experience as the Herald's mouthpiece and this new manifestation. Instead of golden waves, a thick bright channel of light shot down from the sky and poured through Hilthe, emptying out of her chest and into the plaza. Hilthe was the prism through which the Herald's force and power and hungers passed and then took shape again. Slowly, the Herald materialised.

She crouched on the ground, a half-formed figure of lights and limbs. As her strength grew, she clambered to her feet. She resembled Hilthe, as if in passing through she had taken an imprint of the old woman's body, but she was longer and thinner and crueller. Her eyes were bright as diamonds and her lips were black. She was a creature of light and shadow, without nuance, and a star shone on her finger.

No, not a star, Amy realised; it was the ring. As the Herald took shape, the ring seemed to be in two places at once, in the old woman's hands and upon the long alien's finger. As soon as the Herald was wholly present, the light in Hilthe's hands flickered and went out. The ring was gone. The Herald had it now. Hilthe slumped to the ground.

'I have come,' the Herald sang across the valley. 'I have come to claim for my masters what is rightfully theirs!' Seeing the gleaming pile of treasure, the Herald stepped towards it. The excitement in her voice grew. 'We shall be reunited! We shall be restored!'

The Doctor strolled forwards, vulnerable and completely relaxed. 'Hello!' he said. He gave the Herald a little wave. 'Remember me? We chatted earlier.'

The Herald, who had been advancing on the metal, stopped to look at him.

'Remember?' said the Doctor, shielding his eyes from her glare. 'In the hall? Under the dome? You told me about the war. You told me how terrible it was to see your world end. Remember?'

The Herald's black lips parted. 'Yes,' she whispered, the kind of whisper that makes foundations shudder and trees wither.

'Good! Hoped you would!' The Doctor tugged at his ears. 'Memorable face, isn't it? Bit odd, never mind, nothing's for ever. Like wandering about space on your own. How's that working out for you? Must be getting gloomy by now. Tell you what, how would you like to go home?'

The Herald, who had been turning back to the treasure, froze. 'Home,' she breathed.

'It could happen. If you want it to happen. I know how lonely you've been,' the Doctor said, with total honesty. 'I know what it's like, to see the world end, to wander the stars in search of something, anything. But you're not alone. Your species – it's not dead, not by any means! There are so many of them, and they're doing great things! Marvellous things! They're kind people, they work hard, they have a future. You can go back to them. You can be among your own kind again. You can share the peace they're building. You can be a part of it.'

'My home is with my masters. Where they are, I must be. I must be there to serve them.'

'I know you think that. I know you've thought it for a very long time. But it doesn't have to be that way —'

'My masters are coming! They will take back what is theirs! The Bright Nobles will rise again!

They will make a world of light and bliss!'

Amy, remembering that place, shuddered.

The Doctor shook his head. 'I'm sorry,' he said sadly. 'But that isn't going to happen. You have a choice now. You can go home in chains, or you can go home in peace. Either way, it's your home, and it's where you're going. There isn't anywhere else to go.'

'My masters are coming! Our world will be restored!'

'But they're not coming. They can't. They're gone. But you still have somewhere to go. Somewhere much better than the world you lost, much better than wandering alone in the dark, where you're welcome, where you'll be at peace. You've been lost for so long. But everything can change, if you want it to change—'

As the Doctor spoke, a new harmony arose that scorched the air with its intensity. The Herald grew in stature with it. She rose above the valley and stretched out a long and many-fingered hand across it, like an angel of death.

'Liar!' she screamed. 'Deceiver! The Bright Nobles live! They are coming! You cannot hold them back! They will eclipse the sun and boil the sky! This world will burn at their touch! They will break the moon and extinguish your star! The heavens will bear no trace of your existence!' She lifted her hands up towards the dark sky as if in prayer. 'They are coming! They are coming! My masters!'

She lunged at the Doctor.

'Oops,' he said, and dived for cover. As he ran, he slipped and fell to the ground. The Herald moved in, her face raw with rage, her hand raised for the kill…

And Camba came, screaming. Her howl no longer held any note of despair. It was a war cry, a drawing of a line, a challenge to her enemy and a promise of her defeat. She strode across the plaza and with each step she shot up in height. As she bore down upon her enemy, the Doctor scrambled to his feet and dived for cover.

'Don't kill her!' he yelled to Camba. 'You mustn't kill her!'

The Herald moved against her enemy. Amy and Rory took their chance and ran to reach Hilthe. The old woman lay motionless in a dark heap upon the ground. Rory turned her over and Amy cradled her in her arms. 'Please! Wake up! Say something! Be cross about something! Anything!' But Hilthe's eyes stayed shut and her face was bloodless.

Above them, as if the Herald's threat was already coming to pass, the night sky was alight. A great battle unfolded before the people cowering in the city below. Two giants – one ebony, one golden –

clashed like elements from the lowest point of the valley to the highest point amongst the hills. They blazed along the river, seeming almost to set it on fire with the force and fury of their feud. This was a hatred that had lost no intensity even though millennia had passed. The battle was visible for miles around. They saw it in Dant, and they saw it in Sheal, and they talked about it afterwards for centuries.

To Amy, the night seemed endless. Crouched beside the silent dragon, Hilthe cold and lifeless in her arms, she almost despaired of the battle ever ending. The spectacle became too much. She bent over the old woman, leaning in to kiss the top of her head. 'Please,' she whispered to her. 'Don't listen to the music. Stay with us. Stay with me.'

The world crashed into chaos all around her. Then: 'Amy,' Rory whispered. 'Look! Look!' Amy looked. 'It's morning,' Rory said, and took her hand.

Pale dawn light crept into the valley of the Evesh. For a moment, the giants paused in their struggle, marking the change. And then Camba strode forwards and, with the golden sun rising at her back, descended upon her enemy like a cloud of vengeance, extinguishing the Herald's pale light for good. Now turning towards the dawn, Camba lifted her hands to greet the new day and sang her victory out across the valley.

Down in the plaza, Amy and Rory watched fearfully as the Herald shrank down to no more than their height and collapsed on the ground in a heap of long and broken limbs. Camba, shrinking more steadily, stood over her. She took off her helmet and placed it on the ground, and then communicated with her ship in a series of soft clicks and trills. Dark bands, like fetters, appeared around the Herald's thin wrists and ankles and the matter-transmission field took her.

Camba turned and came to kneel beside Hilthe. Gently, she took the old woman's hand within her own long, still gauntleted hands. 'Mother,' she breathed. 'We have her now. She's gone for good. We won.'

As if called back by Camba's words, Hilthe stirred. Her eyelids fluttered open. 'Camba!' she said. 'And the sun too! A long night – and such a strange one!' She lifted Camba's gloved hand and pressed her lips against it. 'My compliments to your mistress – and my grateful thanks to you.'

Camba bowed her head and withdrew. Hilthe closed her eyes again, but Amy could feel warmth returning to her body. She no longer feared for the old woman's life.

Camba communicated once again with her ship. The metal quivered and faded from view. At last, only the dragon remained, its one red eye amused and watchful, its mouth still curved in its secret smile. Then it too trembled and disappeared. A loud, ragged, and undaunted cheer rose up from the plaza.

Hilthe opened her eyes. 'Has it gone?' she said.

'All gone, Mother,' said the Doctor. 'For good.'

'For the best,' Hilthe agreed. 'It was very gaudy. Beautiful, in a certain light. But gaudy.' She closed her eyes again. A party came down from the hall to carry her home.

'I brought you a present,' Amy said to Rory, after Hilthe was safely on her way. 'You know. From the dragon-ship.' She handed over the pen that she had taken from the meeting room. It had a little holographic logo on it. Rory twisted it around in his fingers as if it was the most beautiful thing he had ever seen.

'For me?'

'With love.'

He reached over to kiss her on the cheek. 'Thank you.'

Under the fresh light of the new day, the old city of Geath was at last revealed in all its intricate and diverse design. The buildings were painted in various shades – some honey yellow, some dusty pink, some pale green – and the roofs were covered in terracotta tiles. Complex mosaics in bright stone decorated the street shrines and the fountains, and in the temples candles burned undaunted before bold and ancient frescoes venerating the departed. Floral baskets hung from doorways and archways and, in the long avenues, the trees shifted in the breeze, unburdened of any ornamentation. The dome of the council hall turned out to be made of pale blue glass, the colour of a duck's egg, which tinted the light in the hall and softly washed its white walls and soothed the tempers of those gathered to debate. But the crack across the dome was still there, and the knights remained dead.

The three dead knights – the sum total of the casualties of the only war to come to the valley in over twelve thousand years – were laid to rest with great solemnity in the old burial ground on the western edge of the city. Two of the town's master craftsmen had already begun work on the mosaic that would commemorate them: a redecoration of the whole southern face of the council building around the main doors. Anyone coming to the hall would see it and remember the dead.

The funeral procession passed slowly through the streets. Beol and Hilthe walked together behind the three biers and bystanders showed respect in the traditional way, throwing wild flowers on the stone streets in front of the cortège.

As the bodies went into the ground, Amy saw two dark figures standing some distance away, in the shade of an elderly tree. She tapped the Doctor on the arm. 'Look over there,' she whispered.

Anwa and Camba had come to pay their respects. Seeing they were noticed, Camba lifted her hand and placed it against her chest, in salute. Anwa nodded to the Doctor, who nodded back.

When the ceremony was finished, the Doctor and Amy went to speak to them. Anwa passed the Doctor a little handheld device. 'Interim report,' she said. 'The Herald is in transit to the home world. Her lifeboat has been traced and a division sent to dismantle it. We'll withdraw from local space when that task is complete.' She pointed a long finger to the screen. 'If I could direct you to the bottom of the page, Doctor,' she said. 'You'll see that Protocol Nine Six One has been suspended "pending review". All procedures surrounding first contact are now under review. In fact, I have a conference call on the subject starting in two-tenths.'

'Good.' The Doctor pocketed the report. 'Get it right this time.'

Anwa nodded. Camba saluted them both, and then the matter-transmission field enveloped them, and they were gone.

'Doctor,' Amy said, as they walked back to the

main plaza, 'you still feel sorry for the Herald, don't you?'

The Doctor nodded slowly.

'After all she did. Still you tried to give her a chance for a new life and still she tried to kill you.' Amy shook her head. 'I don't understand you sometimes.'

'Then try to understand her, Amy,' the Doctor said softly. 'Try to glimpse inside her world. The empire she serves comes crashing down. She waits for orders, but her masters are silent. No more commands. No more direction. She doesn't know what to do next. She escapes the last battle, only to wander for centuries, aimlessly, without purpose, alone, waiting for an order that can never come. When she detected some Enamour, it must have been a lifeline. Her world returning at last. But it never could. It's been dead for centuries.'

He stopped walking. He put his hands in his pockets and contemplated the summer day: the green grass, the blue sky, the birdsong, the warm sun, the perpetual present.

'We're done here,' he said. 'Time to go.'

He wasn't quite done. In the main plaza, an envoy from Dant stood before the steps to the council chamber. A neatly dressed and rather jolly man, he stared around quite openly, looking for some sign that might explain the tremendous display in the sky the night before. When he saw Hilthe, he hurried forwards and gave her a smart bow.

'From the citizens of Dant, to our brothers and sisters in Geath, greetings!' he said. 'Mother, a pleasure to see you again!'

Hilthe shook her head. 'I am not the leader of the council,' she said.

'Then to whom should I address myself?' the envoy said. 'Who is the leader now?'

A good question, one to which the citizens of Geath would apply themselves with vigour and enthusiasm over the coming days, as the election approached and the streets and squares filled once again with conversation and debate. For the moment, however, a temporary solution was required so that the visitor might be welcomed properly. Reaching a consensus via some means which Amy could not quite follow, the crowd pulled back and pushed Beol forward. The young man stood blinking at the envoy and then collected himself. 'Well. A most hearty welcome to you. I am… um…'

'Temporarily empowered,' whispered the Doctor in his ear.

'Yes, temporarily empowered to, ah…'

'Speak on behalf of the people of Geath,' the Doctor suggested.

'Speak on behalf of the people of Geath, and,' a light went on behind Beol's eyes and he beckoned to Hilthe to join him, 'my esteemed colleague and I request the pleasure of your company in our hall.'

Beol took Hilthe's arm and, together, they led their guest up the steps into the council building. 'That's more like it!' the Doctor said, beaming at them like he was a match-maker and they were the couple going on the brochure. 'Next on the agenda – electoral reform.'

The travellers left the city in the company of the Teller, travelling in the old cart which had brought him, his brother, and the dragon into Geath all those months earlier.

'Why aren't you staying?' Amy asked the Teller. 'Now that your brother is… well, whatever he is now?'

'I think I've outstayed my welcome in Geath,' the Teller said. 'Besides, who there is going to listen to a tale about a king and a dragon?'

They travelled along the wide road that led out of Geath and then, more bumpily, along a muddy track. Rory, sitting in the back of the cart, caught a glimpse of metal beneath the canvas cover thrown over the Teller's possessions. His heart nearly stopped. Surely the Teller hadn't been foolish enough to keep a scrap of Enamour? Would he even realise if he had? Glancing round to make sure that nobody was watching, Rory twitched the canvas aside.

Underneath lay the little satellite dish, black and silver and mercifully Enamour-free. Rory put the canvas back and said nothing. No harm done and, anyway, the Teller had earned it.

'Here we are!' called the Doctor from up front.

The cart trundled to a halt. They all clambered down and went off into the trees. Soon they saw the TARDIS, solid and safe, waiting patiently for them in the forest. The Teller stared at it and the Doctor preened.

'Oh, you just love this bit, don't you?' said Amy. To the Teller, she said, 'What are you going to do now?'

The Teller shook himself. 'I don't know. Keep travelling, I suppose, keep telling stories…'

'You should make some up about a man who travels in time and space—'

'Doctor,' Amy said in a warning voice, 'it's not always about you.'

The Doctor looked at her as if he literally did not understand the words coming from her mouth.

'How?' said the Teller. '*How* do you all fit in there?'

'Oh, you know,' said the Doctor, opening the TARDIS door and waving his hand about vaguely.

'Magic. Sort of. In all the ways that count.'

Inside the TARDIS, it was as peaceable and timeless as ever. On the monitor, Amy and Rory watched the Teller walk all the way round the blue box. He stopped in front of the doors and shook his head. Then he burst out laughing.

Amy laughed too. 'I wonder what story he'll make out of all this?' she said. 'I wonder what it will come out like?'

'Farce, probably,' said Rory drily.

'Hey!' Amy punched him gently on the arm. 'I thought there were scary bits.'

'Of course, it's all a question of emphasis,' the Doctor put in quietly. 'If you think about it, a dragon can mean anything – facing your fears, maybe, or not being taken in by appearances...' He looked down at the TARDIS console and gave a secret sombre smile. 'It can even be a reminder that although it's within your power to force people to do what's best for them, you shouldn't.' His finger hovered over a button. 'Least, not often.' He hit the control, and the TARDIS dematerialised. Their last sight was of the Teller's expression: sheer joy at hearing the best sound in the universe.

The Doctor turned to his friends. 'Pockets,' he said briskly.

'Pockets?' said Rory.

'I bet we all picked up a souvenir or two.'

One by one they checked. The Doctor placed the ring that had summoned the Herald onto the TARDIS console. Rory surrendered the circular tile that Hilthe had given him. Amy took out the spoon she had lifted from the gatekeeper's house. She held it for a moment, warm and tingling in the palm of her hand, and then shuddered and relinquished it.

'What are we going to do with the stuff, Doctor?' she said. 'Are we going to destroy it?'

The Doctor shook his head. 'You can't destroy knowledge,' he said softly. 'You can't un-make it; you can't un-know it. You can only use it – and do your best not to let it use you.' He dug deep into his pocket again. He pulled out a fork and threw it on top of the little pile of treasure. Then he turned away and set to at the controls, pulling and pushing indeterminate levers and buttons. A silver haze surrounded the objects and they disappeared from sight.

'Goodbye Enamour,' said Rory, his tone a combination of relief and regret.

Amy took hold of his hand. The TARDIS moved on.

Only the metal remained, glowing palely in the vacuum of space.

Acknowledgements

Grateful thanks to Gary Russell, Steve Tribe, and particularly Justin Richards for advice and enthusiasm. Big thanks also to Oli Smith for chat and encouragement during writing. And thank you, as always, to Matthew.

Available now from BBC Books:

DOCTOR ⬛ WHO

Apollo 23

by Justin Richards

£6.99 ISBN 978 1 846 07200 0

An astronaut in full spacesuit appears out of thin air in a busy shopping centre. Maybe it's a publicity stunt.

A photo shows a well-dressed woman in a red coat lying dead at the edge of a crater on the dark side of the moon – beside her beloved dog 'Poochie'. Maybe it's a hoax.

But, as the Doctor and Amy find out, these are just minor events in a sinister plan to take over every human being on Earth. The plot centres on a secret military base on the moon – that's where Amy and the TARDIS are.

The Doctor is back on Earth, and without the TARDIS there's no way he can get to the moon to save Amy and defeat the aliens.

Or is there? The Doctor discovers one last great secret that could save humanity: Apollo 23.

A thrilling, all-new adventure featuring the Doctor and Amy, as played by Matt Smith and Karen Gillan in the spectacular hit series from BBC Television.

Available now from BBC Books:

DOCTOR WHO
The Forgotten Army
by Brian Minchin

£6.99 ISBN 978 1 846 07987 0

New York – one of the greatest cities on 21st-century Earth... But what's going on in the Museum? And is that really a Woolly Mammoth rampaging down Broadway?

An ordinary day becomes a time of terror, as the Doctor and Amy meet a new and deadly enemy. The vicious Army of the Vykoid are armed to the teeth and determined to enslave the human race. Even though they're only seven centimetres high.

With the Vykoid army swarming across Manhattan and sealing it from the world with a powerful alien force field, Amy has just 24 hours to find the Doctor and save the city. If she doesn't, the people of Manhattan will be taken to work in the doomed asteroid mines of the Vykoid home planet.

But as time starts to run out, who can she trust? And how far will she have to go to free New York from the Forgotten Army?

A thrilling, all-new adventure featuring the Doctor and Amy, as played by Matt Smith and Karen Gillan in the spectacular hit series from BBC Television.

Available now from BBC Books:

DOCTOR ᛜ WHO
Nuclear Time

by Oli Smith

£6.99 ISBN 978 1 846 07989 4

Colorado, 1981. The Doctor, Amy and Rory arrive in Appletown – an idyllic village in the remote American desert where the townsfolk go peacefully about their suburban routines. But when two more strangers arrive, things begin to change.

The first is a mad scientist – whose warnings are cut short by an untimely and brutal death. The second is the Doctor...

As death falls from the sky, the Doctor is trapped. The TARDIS is damaged, and the Doctor finds he is living backwards through time. With Amy and Rory being hunted through the suburban streets of the Doctor's own future and getting farther away with every passing second, he must unravel the secrets of Appletown before time runs out...

A thrilling, all-new adventure featuring the Doctor, Amy and Rory, as played by Matt Smith, Karen Gillan and Arthur Darvill in the spectacular hit series from BBC Television.

Coming soon from BBC Books:

DOCTOR WHO

The Only Good Dalek

by Justin Richards and Mike Collins

£16.99 ISBN 978 1 846 07984 9

Station 7 is where the Earth Forces send all the equipment captured in their unceasing war against the Daleks. It's where Dalek technology is analysed and examined. It's where the Doctor and Amy have just arrived. But somehow the Daleks have found out about Station 7 – and there's something there that they want back.

With the Doctor increasingly worried about the direction the Station's research is taking, the commander of Station 7 knows he has only one possible, desperate, defence. Because the last terrible secret of Station 7 is that they don't only store captured Dalek technology. It's also a prison. And the only thing that might stop a Dalek is another Dalek…

An epic, full-colour graphic novel featuring the Doctor and Amy, as played by Matt Smith and Karen Gillan in the spectacular hit series from BBC Television.